AN HEIRLOOM CHRISTMAS

MEGAN SQUIRES

*For everyone who stills believes
in the magic of Christmas.*

CHRISSY

"I'M NOT SURE I want this masterpiece hanging on anyone's door but my own!"

Doris lowered her tortoiseshell reading glasses to peer over their rim as she held her wreath at arm's length to survey her craftsmanship. Predictably, she'd opted for a coffee theme this year, with plastic mugs adhered to the floral wire and letters that read, *'But First, Coffee!'* arching over the top. Given that Doris Beasley and her husband, Earl, owned the only coffee shop in Heirloom Point, it was an expected choice.

Nita O'Dell, the other half of the LOL's—or *Little Old Ladies* as they'd coined themselves years before—stuck to a more traditional holiday theme. She'd adorned her wreath with holly berries, an expertly tied wire-ribbon bow, and mistletoe sprigs tucked into the pine branches. Even with the classic theme, her wreath was anything but generic.

Chrissy Davenport would be proud to display either

on her front door and she knew she would have the hardest time choosing at the upcoming *Silent Night Silent Auction*. This event was a favorite Heirloom Point tradition, something she counted down to each year, crossing off the days on her calendar as they led up to the month of December. It was a town-wide celebration where everyone gathered to bid on Christmas wreaths in an effort to raise money for charity.

This year, all proceeds would go to the brand new children's wing at the local hospital. Chrissy had participated as a young girl, often working alongside her mother, until she was finally old enough to design her own wreath to enter in the auction. The nostalgia of that tradition filled Chrissy with holiday spirit like no other celebration could. And today was November 30th; just one more satisfying stroke of her red marker on her calendar until the exchange officially kicked off. She could hardly wait!

"Nice choice with the flocking, Everleigh. Makes it feel so wintery," Chrissy said, nodding her head toward her sister's handiwork. Everleigh squinted her eyes, the tip of her tongue darting through her lips as she narrowed all concentration on the glue gun in one hand, the snowman ornament in the other.

"Shhh," Everleigh hushed, eyebrows scrunching together. "I need complete focus here. I only recently formed a new fingerprint after last year's hot glue snafu. Sizzled that sucker right off!"

"Could be convenient if you've got a warrant out for your arrest," Doris noted aloud, still eyeing her wreath over glasses that she used more for fashion than function. She was the smaller of the two LOL's, petite in stature in an almost elfish way. But she had the mightiest personality, no question about that. She was often even more boisterous than the caffeinated coffee drinkers that frequented her shop in the town's square. "One less fingerprint equals one less way to confirm your guilt."

"With a police officer for a dad in a town where everyone knows everyone else's business, no chance of that!" With a contented grunt, Everleigh secured the figurine onto her wreath. "Plus, I'm not the one with a law breaking background. Let's not forget the time my older and much more criminally-inclined sister spent the night in the slammer." She nudged Chrissy with her elbow.

"I was *barely* eighteen. Practically still a kid," Chrissy retorted.

"The law doesn't care how many hours into adulthood you are when you break it. Illegal is illegal, even if it was technically just trespassing."

"If my memory serves me correctly," Doris began, "and at my age it often doesn't, so take this with a heaping spoonful of salt—wasn't Nick McHenry truly to blame for that little incident?"

The fine hairs on Chrissy's neck bristled at the name. For nearly a decade, she'd only heard it spoken through the echo of her television speakers or read it typed as a headline on the Heirloom Point Post. The town was good at celebrating Nick's victories, but also took note of his shortcomings. Wasn't it always the tragedy that garnered all of the attention, all of the publicity? It was as though there was some inexplicable pleasure gained in watching a person's fall from success. Not that Nick had any real say in his sudden and swift departure from the limelight. Despite his failings, he was ever the hometown hero. To everyone except Chrissy, that was.

"Sure. Nick was *totally* to blame," Everleigh snorted, sarcasm thick like peanut butter in her tone. "Just like he was to blame for that career ending knee injury that had him out the majority of last season."

"I heard he's making a permanent move back to Heirloom Point, you know," Nita spoke up, her Minnesota roots revealed in the timbre of her voice. She was much meeker than her LOL counterpart, grandmotherly and warm. "I almost can't believe it. Retired at the ripe old age of thirty. I guess years as a professional hockey player are calculated in dog years." She giggled.

If the mention of Nick's name gave her chills, this information made Chrissy go white hot with panic. Watching Nick compete on the ice rink from her living room couch was vastly different than seeing him walk through Heirloom Point Square. She wasn't sure what she would do if she bumped into him during an afternoon of holiday shopping, or worse yet, if he stopped into his parents' hardware store located directly across from her own little candle shop. She had so many things she wanted to say to him—a myriad of questions and as many pointed assertions—but she figured in that moment, she'd fall instantly mute.

"Do you two still keep in touch, sweetie?" Nita asked.

Everleigh shot a brief, knowing glance toward

Chrissy, then turned to the older women at their shared craft table. She spoke on her sister's behalf. "Chrissy and Nick? Oh, come on LOL's. That news is older than the light bulb in Chrissy's store window; you all know that."

"And just how many years has that bulb been on now?" Doris asked, head tilted. She finally slipped the unnecessary glasses from her pert nose and settled them onto the table. "Would you believe I remember seeing it when I was a young girl, always shining and sparkling in that front display. Almost magical, when you think of it."

"As the story goes, it's been illuminated for seventy-four years and counting, minus the occasional power outage," Chrissy answered, more than grateful for the change in topic. Plus, she always loved talking about her shop and its quirky eccentricities. It was absolutely filled with them. "It'll hit the seventy-five year mark this holiday season. I think that deserves a storewide sale!"

"Isn't it amazing"—Doris winked directly at Chrissy, a deliberately long blink that served as a signal—"that something could still burn brightly after *all of these years*? Some things really do withstand the test of time."

Chrissy picked up on the double meaning, but it wasn't just time that had pulled Nick and Chrissy apart. Even though she'd tried to get out of the conversation which had suddenly spun full circle, she hadn't been successful. Rising to stand, she collected her wreath from the table. "I think I'm all done with this one. I've managed to fill every inch of it and I worry if I add anything else, it'll be too heavy to even hang on a door!"

"I've got a few more embellishments to add before

mine's auction worthy." Everleigh grabbed ahold of the hot glue gun, wincing. "Shoot!" She thrust her thumb into her mouth to soothe the new burn. "Another one bites the dust."

"I think you've officially started your own tradition, sis." Chrissy patted the crown of Everleigh's blonde curls, so different from the sleek, auburn strands that fanned out just above her own shoulders. "I must say," she noted, looking at the Christmas wreath she'd spent all morning crafting, "I'm truly pleased with my work this year. I'm curious to see whose door it'll end up on."

"Won't be mine!" Doris exclaimed with a barking laugh. "I'm not bidding on yours this year, or any year, for that matter. In fact, I'd pay good money for you to keep it!"

"That's just cruel, Doris." Chrissy clutched her chest with her free hand, feigning offense.

Doris shook her head, making a *tsk-tsk* sound between her teeth. "I'm still trying to recover from that awful bout of fruitcake food poisoning, I'll have you know."

"I thought it was a nice gesture to bake a sweet treat for the highest bidder of my wreath," Chrissy said. "As I recall, you did pay a pretty penny for it."

"And my digestive system paid an even higher price," Doris deadpanned.

Chrissy shrugged. "Isn't it sort of an unspoken rule to give a little thank you gift to the winner of your wreath, anyway? I mean, I think that's the only reason Dad bids on Miss Sandra's every year. Her wreaths are hardly spectacular. He's in it purely for the legendary apple streusel she takes down to the station the day after the auction. Makes the holidays feel even cozier when you really engage with your neighbors and get into the gift giving spirit, doesn't it?"

"Of course! And I can imagine it would feel even cozier if your highest bidder was someone you were technically *engaged* to at one point in time." Doris flashed Chrissy a sideways glance that made Chrissy feel as though her stomach had bottomed out.

Hugging her wreath close to her body, Chrissy pretended she didn't hear that last comment. She couldn't let her heart settle into a discussion that involved Nick, even if it was just about a silly wreath. In fact, she often found herself bowing out of any conversation that merely mentioned his name. Avoidance was her go-to whenever Nick was involved.

Taking a backward step toward the community center's automatic doors, Chrissy said her quick goodbyes and made her way for the exit. She admired the finished wreaths spread out on the tables like delicately iced sugar cookies cooling on a tray. By the looks of it, this year promised to bring in more bids than all previous years combined. The number of town participants was at an all time high. That very thought made Chrissy's heart swell with pride in her community and gratefulness for the generous donations she knew the hospital would receive this holiday as a result of the auction. She couldn't wait until it was her turn to select a wreath from among the beautiful handiworks.

She also couldn't help but wonder which neighbor would choose her wreath this year, knowing deep down it wouldn't be Nick McHenry like the LOL's predicted.

Nick made his choice many years ago, and it was clear it would never be Chrissy.

NICK

❄

"THANK YOU, MR. Davies. This will be perfect."

Nick McHenry surveyed the eight-hundred square foot in-law quarters, sensing in one sweeping glance that it had everything he could possibly need. He even noted the Italian manufactured espresso maker on the counter, a luxury he never afforded himself in his previous bachelor pad. Not that he even knew how to use a complex machine like that. Fancy coffees weren't really his thing. In fact, he was more of a smoothie drinking guy, often hiding the leafy greens his personal trainer insisted he eat in something more appealing.

"You don't have to call me Mr. Davies, Nick. It's been over ten years since you were my student. Robert will be just fine."

"Not sure I'll be able to do that, sir," Nick admitted. It would be a hard habit to break. Reconnecting with his high school teacher brought back that dreaded *unpre-*

pared-on-test-day panic. Instantly, he'd transported to his teenage years. It wasn't just the sight of his old geometry teacher that took him on that journey through time, though. The moment his truck tires rolled over the Heirloom Point county line, every memory from his youth rushed in like a break in a levee.

But the rented space on Mr. Davies's property was uncharted territory and the unfamiliarity of it was refreshing, like a crisp sheet of blank paper, ready for a new story to be penned. It was hard to find something that didn't hold the many memories Nick had tried to stuff down over the last decade. As he expected they would, his parents had offered his old bedroom when he first broke the news of his homecoming. However, the thought of a grown man living in a room that boasted rock band posters and a bookcase full of youth hockey trophies didn't sit well with Nick. Things were different now— even if they felt remarkably the same—and he couldn't go back to the life he'd lived before in Heirloom Point. He had to make a new one. He had no choice but to start over.

"You're more than welcome to join us for dinner, Nick," Robert Davies said, standing in the doorframe, readying to go. "Pamela's got a lasagna baking in the oven and I'm headed to the store to grab the forgotten bag of salad I promised to bring home on my way from school. There will be plenty to go around if you're hungry."

"I appreciate the invite, but I already told my folks I'd swing by later on tonight. Mom's video calling Kevin and she has this whole plan for a family dinner around the table. We haven't had a real one in years," Nick explained. "I'd love to take a rain check on dinner, though. Home cooked meals are at the very top of the *things I missed most about home* list."

"Rain check it is." Robert smacked his hand against the open door, almost as a high five. "Go ahead and get settled in. Pamela and I will give you your space, but please don't hesitate to reach out if you need anything. We're here and happy to help." Tipping his head and stepping over the threshold onto the small front stoop, Robert said, "Good to have you back in Heirloom Point, Nick."

"Good to be back, sir."

And it was good. For the most part. Around ninety-five percent good. The leftover five percent, though, that little sliver wasn't good. It wasn't bad, necessarily, it was just this wedge of uncertainty that wouldn't let Nick slip into feeling entirely *good* about his move back home. Several things fell into that five percent portion, but namely Chrissy Davenport.

At one point in time, she had been Nick's everything. His one hundred percent. He'd always told her that, too, and she'd argued that she couldn't be his everything if hockey was also his everything. You couldn't have two everythings. But Nick never compartmentalized things that way—not until now with his five percent slice of doubt that suddenly felt much larger the more he dwelled on it.

In fact, the longer he stood in the middle of his rented home, his chest compressed with apprehension and unease, the more those percentages slid all around. Maybe coming back to Heirloom Point was a toss up, a fifty-fifty sort of situation. People would either be glad about his homecoming, or they wouldn't. But even if all of the town's population was happy to have Nick back and Chrissy wasn't, it would still feel wrong to be there.

How Chrissy could still have that much influence over his emotions bewildered Nick. They'd called things off abruptly; a clean break. No looking back. It was a decision they had made together, neither encouraging nor discouraging it more than the other. It was simply the only reasonable thing to do and they were both logical people.

Even still, the fact that they hadn't communicated for ten full years floored Nick when he let his mind linger on that reality. The first few days were the hardest, but he had forced it into an out of sight, out of mind thing. As the days stacked one on top of the other, it became almost natural to go without speaking. It was like creating a new habit—how it took several weeks of discipline and deter-mination to change one's ways.

Nick had to create the habit of living a life without Chrissy Davenport in it.

When he was drafted to the Newcastle Northern Lights, he almost fell off that wagon. His fingers had dialed her phone number—all but the very last digit—without even intending to. It was like playing a piano song memorized in childhood, your fingers knowing the notes and plunking them out on their own accord. Instinctually, almost.

It had been instinct to want to share that news with Chrissy. He had wanted to tell her first, before she saw it as the newspaper headline, those big block letters detached of feeling. They couldn't convey the emotion that was so weighty in that life-changing announcement.

It had been Nick's childhood dream to play in the NHL. As a young boy learning to skate on old Prosper Tomlin's frozen pond during Heirloom Point's lengthy winters, he'd envisioned himself competing in an arena as a part of the Newcastle Northern Lights. One year for Christmas, Chrissy had saved up all of her hard-earned money from working at Nick's parents' store as an after school job, using it to purchase a pre-owned, Dusty Hayforth Northern Lights jersey off the internet for Nick. It was visibly well-worn before it even got into his hands, but the sacrifice Chrissy made to buy that jersey made Nick's heart turn to mush. If he hadn't already been head-over-heels for the sweet seventeen-year-old with wavy dark hair that smelled of springtime, that gesture would've catapulted him into full-on love. He wore that jersey his entire junior year of high school, until the stitching came completely off of the number 9 patch and it dangled by a thread.

Thinking about it now, Nick wondered where that jersey ended up throughout his many travels. Likely stuffed in a dust-covered shipping box in his storage unit. Glancing across the room at the two lone suitcases of belongings, Nick questioned if it had been a wise decision to leave so many of his things back in Newcastle. He figured it was a dropped anchor, something to pull him back to that city even though hockey—the one thing that first drew him there—no longer held a place in his life.

As if on cue, his knee began to ache, that dull but persistent discomfort he'd grown to ignore, like the annoyance of an untreated toothache or burrowed splinter. Rubbing his scar with his fingers, he closed his eyes and drew in a breath through clenched teeth. The surgery had been a full year prior. Even though the doctors remarked how well he'd healed, Nick sensed he'd never be quite the same. His terminated contract with the Northern Lights was all the proof he'd needed to solidify that hunch.

Rolling his shoulders, he shook his head and lumbered forward, careful not to put his full weight on his left leg. He'd been assured it was "good as new," but Nick could easily recall the enormity of that terrifying injury. Whether he intended to or not, he favored that leg and likely always would.

With slow strides, he hobbled his way to the kitchen. Nick glanced at the espresso machine and resolved to learn how to use it that holiday season. There was likely a video tutorial online that would have him whipping up mochas like a barista in no time. The last woman he had briefly dated always ordered the most complex coffee drinks, like she was reciting a Shakespearean monologue rather than ordering a caffeinated beverage. But a few of the drinks actually sounded decent, especially the peppermint mocha he'd stolen a sip of when they'd caroled on the coldest of Newcastle nights. Maybe Nick could learn to like new things, fluffy coffee drinks being the first on the list. It seemed like an easily achievable victory, and Nick was in desperate need of a victory, in whatever form it presented itself.

Familiarizing himself with the new space, he looked around, noting the matching sugar and creamer ceramics on the counter to the left of the machine and a Mason jar candle on the right. He reached out for the candle and took it into his grip, unscrewing the metal ring to release the lid with his other hand. Like a spray of perfume, the aroma of honeysuckle and vanilla wafted around him. The candle almost slipped from his grasp, the scent smacking his senses awake.

He was suddenly twenty-years-old again, sitting in the bed of his truck, his high school letterman jacket slipped over Chrissy's narrow shoulders, his nose pressed softly into her hair. Inhaling deeply, Nick could feel his heart pick up speed within his chest, quickening just like it had on that autumn evening when he'd uttered the question that forever changed him. Forever changed them.

Today had been an afternoon of time travel for Nick, that candle being the biggest transporter of them all. Curious, he tipped it upside down, looking for a label.

Chrissy's Candle Company.

Setting the candle onto the granite, he deliberated only a brief moment before grabbing a matchbook from the counter. He struck the tip against the sandpaper, lit the wick, and gave in to the fact that every square inch of Heirloom Point was bound and determined to pull him into the past, once and for all.

CHRISSY

C HRISSY LIKED TO have complete quiet while candle making. She needed her senses to zero in on the various oils and combinations of fragrances, no other distractions vying for her attention. It was similar to turning down the car radio when trying to locate a destination on her GPS. It didn't make any sense, but somehow it always worked.

She'd gotten into the shop early that morning, just before sunrise. Chrissy needed the entire shop to herself during these waning moments before daylight. Once Everleigh clocked in, it would be nonstop chatter straight through until lunchtime, and likely during that, too. While she loved her sister's company and the help she provided at the shop, Chrissy coveted these precious few hours of calm when she could do her best and most focused work.

Today's goal was to create the annual Christmas

candle. She'd gathered her favorite festive oils from the shelf: clove, pine, cedar wood, and sugar. She wanted both the warm, welcoming smell of Grandma's Christmas kitchen, coupled with the nostalgic aroma of freshly cut evergreen trees. It was a difficult balance to achieve and she'd been at it for two hours without landing on the right blend. Every attempted mixture reminded her of the previous year's candle—*Balsam and Bells*—and she'd be darned to repeat it. Where was the creativity in rerunning the past?

She knew her friends and family eagerly awaited the launch of her holiday candle. It was fun to watch their faces when they lifted the lid for the first time and pulled in a deep, intentional breath. It was like watching a loved one unwrap a long awaited gift on Christmas morning. There was joy and contentment and warmth and cheer. In a way, it felt as though—without even intending to—Chrissy had created her very own Heirloom Point tradition. She loved that anyone had the ability to do that. Though the word itself hinted at longevity, all traditions needed a true starting point. Chrissy was so grateful for her little shop and the starting point it afforded all of her dreams and ambitions.

By the time the sun crested through the store's windows at daybreak, washing the candle displays with hazy, golden light, Chrissy had decided to call it quits on that particular creative session. No combination of scents felt like the right one. She tidied up her workstation just as the store's entrance door chimed upon opening.

Expecting it to be Everleigh, she startled when she heard a low, baritone voice instead.

"Morning!" a man called out as the door swung shut, rattling the chime once more as it settled into place.

"I'm back here!"

Chrissy could hear the footfalls of thick boots and when he rounded the corner to her small workshop in the rear of the building, she beamed at the sight of her father dressed in his police officer's uniform, ready to begin his day.

As a young girl, Chrissy always admired her father in uniform. He looked proud and strong and even though the recent years had been trying, her father always wore a resilient smile on his weathered face. He was noticeably handsome, with short graying hair shaved closely on the sides, left just a smidge longer on top. A thick, neat mustache ran the length of his upper lip and two dimples indented his cheeks even when he wasn't fully grinning, like they were just waiting to deepen with a smile. Of the two daughters, Chrissy favored her father looks-wise, her dimples the most noticeable match. Everleigh had their mom's signature golden curls, and even though she tried not to, Chrissy always felt a twinge of jealousy over that. Oh how she'd wanted the image in her mirror to reflect the likeness of her mother, even just a bit. She often wondered what it would be like to visibly carry around a piece of her mom in her own appearance.

"Smells wonderful in here, Chrissy," Lee said, leaning over to kiss his daughter on her forehead. He picked up a small bottle of oil from the wooden tabletop and rolled it between two fingers. "Working on your holiday candle?"

"I can't get it right, Dad. I've been at it all morning and I feel like everything I mix smells just like last year's."

"I liked last year's candle," her father said.

"So did I, but I want to create something new. Something different."

Her dad shrugged. "I think what people appreciate about your candles is the comfort found in them. How the scents take them back to a certain time or place in their memory." Dropping two hands onto his daughter's shoulders and squeezing lightly, he said, "I know that's what I love about them."

Chrissy stood from her metal stool and took her father's hand to walk with him out into the store. It wasn't more than four hundred square feet or so in total, with a tiny back area where she did most of her candle making and bookkeeping. She'd portioned off sections of the open space with distressed cabinets, bookshelves, and tables, creating little cubbies to display her fragrant products.

This time of year, the shop transformed into a winter wonderland, complete with garland swags draped over every surface and miniature evergreen trees decked out with twinkling lights and small silver balls on their branches. She'd used the softest fleece fabric she'd ever touched to create a carpet of "snow" in the front window display and she'd sprayed white Styrofoam balls with iridescent paint, arranging them as snowballs strewn about. It was like stepping into a scene from the North Pole, and Chrissy just loved it.

"Moved things around a bit since I was last in?" Lee squinted as his searching gaze swept over the shop.

Chrissy knew just what he was looking for. She walked toward the closest shelf and pulled down a coral tinted candle, then handed it to her father.

He lifted the lid from the glass jar, his eyes slipping softly shut as he breathed in the sweet, flowery aroma. Chrissy watched his mouth purse as though holding back something he chose not to say, and when he opened his eyes, a reflective sheen of tears collected in them.

"It's like a piece of her is still here, Chrissy. Seriously, it smells just like her." His words floated out on a breath. "*Just* like her."

After her mother's passing three years earlier, Chrissy made it her mission to make a candle that emulated the floral-scented perfume her mom dabbed onto her wrists and neck each morning. Rose and honey-suckle and almond with just the smallest hint of cherry blossom. Chrissy couldn't believe she was able to match it so closely. It was remarkable, really—a gift almost. That was the only real explanation for it: there was just a bit of divine intervention involved in creating that particularly meaningful scent.

Every time her father came into the store, he'd take the candle from the display, open it, and breathe in the cherished memories of his beloved wife, Audrey. It was the perfect, calming start to his otherwise hectic day.

"I'll say it again, but you are more than welcome to

take one home with you, Dad," Chrissy said. "I have plenty to spare and can always make more. That's one recipe I have memorized."

"You know why I like keeping it here, Chrissy."

And she did. Not only did the candle remind everyone of Audrey Davenport, the entire store embodied her. After all, when Chrissy opened it, she and her mother were partners in the venture. She couldn't even count how many early mornings they'd spent together, mixing and breathing in candle concoctions until they were dizzy from the strong fragrances and delirious from hours of laughter. For that reason, the store would always hold the deepest place in Chrissy's heart, especially those early dawn hours. It was practically her home away from home.

Lee placed the candle back onto the shelf, just as the door to the shop burst open, a startling swirl of frosty air blasting into the space like a freezer door thrown open.

"It's gonna be a cold one!" Everleigh bellowed, tumbling into the shop with snowball-like momentum. She ran her palms up and down her arms vigorously before unwinding her plaid scarf from around her neck and bunching it up in her hands. "We either need to light every candle in this store for warmth or crank up that heater! We'll be icicles by the end of the day if we don't!"

"Heater's still on the fritz, sis." Chrissy reached out for Everleigh's quilted jacket. She folded it over her arm as soon as her sister slipped it off. "I've got a call into Ted, but we're not the only ones in Heirloom Point with HVAC needs. We'll have to wait our turn."

"I'm happy to take a look at it after my shift. In the meantime, the McHenry's probably have a space heater you could use. Don't think one would cost you more than fifty dollars, tops," Lee suggested.

It wasn't as though that thought hadn't crossed Chrissy's mind a half dozen times already. Of course the hardware store would have one. In fact, she knew they had at least two different models in their selection. From her time spent as a store employee during her teenage years, Chrissy would probably even be able to locate the heaters without any assistance. Aisle thirteen, right next to the air purifiers and oscillating fans.

But she wasn't about to march across the street and buy one. Not with Nick back in town.

"We'll be just fine, Dad. They're not predicting snow until later this evening."

"If the snow starts falling and we still don't have heat, I'm officially quitting." Hands on her hips, Everleigh jutted her bottom lip just like she did as a child. Chrissy was well acquainted with that look, the one that got her younger sister off the hook more times than was reasonable. Unlike her parents, Chrissy was immune to its influence.

"It would certainly be a shame to lose you right before the holiday rush, but Nita did say she's looking for part time work. Might be the perfect time to bring her on. When's your last day?"

Squiggling her mouth into a grimace, Everleigh swatted her sister. "You know I'll never leave you."

"Is that a threat?" Chrissy teased, her voice breaking into a laugh on the last syllable.

"Alright girls, as much as I'd love to stay and listen to you two bicker all day, duty calls. Someone has to keep the citizens of Heirloom Point in line, and today, that someone is me."

"In that case, wouldn't it fall under your job description to referee our arguments and keep *us* in line?" Everleigh teased.

"I've already put in my time doing just that. Officially retired from that position the day you moved out." Lee rubbed his palms, one against the other, as though wiping them clean of his parental responsibilities.

"And boomerang! I'm baaaack!" Everleigh singsonged. Reaching out for a hug, she wrapped her arms around her father and squeezed. "Be safe out there today."

"Always try to be," Lee said, pulling out of Everleigh's firm embrace and turning to give his eldest daughter a hug before heading toward the door. "Will you both be at the silent auction tonight? I'll be busy working security, but I hope to see you there."

"Absolutely!" they spoke in unplanned unison.

Laughing, Lee grabbed the door handle and exited the shop, tossing one last wave over his shoulder as he stepped onto the sidewalk of Spruce Street.

Everleigh spun toward her sister. "So, how's the new candle coming along?"

"It's not," Chrissy answered, resignation heavy in her tone.

"You put too much thought into it, you know."

"I put too much heart into it, I think," Chrissy corrected. "But I don't think that's necessarily a bad thing. Just makes the process a little longer than I'd prefer. I should've started weeks ago, honestly."

"You already know I don't have the best sniffer, but I'm happy to lend my nose if you need it."

Everleigh wasn't exaggerating; she had a terrible sense of smell. Just a few months earlier, Chrissy thought it would be fun to do a blind testing of sorts. She had peeled the labels from the jars and blindfolded her sister, then instructed her to note the various scented oils within each candle. To say it was a miss was a gross understatement. Everleigh had the worst nose of anyone she'd ever met. Suddenly nutmeg was cinnamon and basil was mint and peach was pear. It was all a messy mixture of wrong ingredients, to a laughable degree. While it was undeniable that Everleigh was an excellent saleswoman, she failed miserably when it came to fragrance identification.

"I'll figure it out," Chrissy said, grateful for her sister's offer even still. "It'll come to me. Always does. I just need to pick a scent and run with it."

"Speaking of picking things, have you thought about which wreath you might pick tonight? I've got my eye on Trisha Lancing's this year. It's a candy cane wreath, Chrissy! The ones they make at their candy shoppe down the street. I heard there are over three hundred, full-sized candy canes on it! I figure even if it goes for upwards of fifty bucks, it'll still be a screaming deal!"

"I haven't thought too much about what I'm looking

for this year. I'm sure once I see something I like, I'll just go for it."

"Something else you might like..." Everleigh's voice trailed off as her gaze slid over the shop and out the front window. She nudged her chin in the same direction.

There, on the sidewalk of Spruce Street, directly across from Chrissy's Candle Company, was Nick McHenry, walking through the square as though he'd never even left.

Chrissy dropped to the floor.

"What on earth are you doing?" Everleigh shouted.

"Shhh!" Grabbing her sister's sleeve, Chrissy yanked her down to her level.

"Why are we hiding?" Everleigh whispered this time as she crouched onto the wooden floorboards. "He can't see us."

"He might be able to."

Popping her head up over the table, Everleigh squinted. "Nope. He just went into McHenry Hardware. The coast is totally clear."

Falling back on her haunches, Chrissy slumped against the bookcase and closed her eyes, relief filling her like helium in a balloon.

"Is this the reaction I can expect from a Nick sighting? Because I have a sneaking suspicion he'll be helping his family out at the store a lot this holiday season. If flattening onto the floor is going to be your response, I need to invest in some knee pads. I can't be diving for cover like this without a little protection."

Chrissy smacked her forehead with her palm, admittedly embarrassed by her overreaction. "Why am I acting like this, Ev? I mean, seriously. Why am I so terrified to see him again?"

"My best guess would be the fear of the unknown."

"But I know Nick." Chrissy paused. "Or at least I *knew* him. I mean, I knew him better than anyone. Didn't I?"

"Are you worried he's not the same guy?"

"I think I'm actually worried he is."

Everleigh's expression changed, a look of empathy molding her features. Reaching out, she smoothed a wayward strand of dark hair that had fallen across her sister's forehead. "Okay, then. Let's come up with some sort of warning for when we do see him—like a type of Nick radar. Something associated with him but not too closely, so we don't give it away. What was that word he always used for the hockey puck back in high school?"

"The puck? Wasn't it biscuit?"

"Yes!" Everleigh nodded. "That'll be our code word. Biscuit!" she yelled, megaphoning her mouth as she cupped her hands on either side.

"You are the world's biggest dork. You know that, right?"

"If that's your way of saying I'm the world's best sister, then *thankyouverymuch*," Everleigh said, beaming a broad, toothy grin.

"I'm not sure how I feel about biscuits," Chrissy said. She gained enough confidence to peek over the tabletop to scope out the situation on the street. All was clear, as far as she could tell. Cautiously, she rose to her feet.

"Yeah. Biscuits are confusing," Everleigh said as she stood up, too.

Chrissy laughed, thankful for her younger sister and her uncanny ability to make every situation more manageable.

"We're not actually talking about real biscuits, right?" Everleigh confirmed, a pained look spreading onto her face. "Because those are absolutely delicious. Nothing confusing about that."

"Just the hockey related ones," Chrissy clarified. "Buttermilk biscuits are completely fine."

"Maybe you've just landed on a scent for your new holiday candle? Jingle Bell Buttermilk Biscuit? Is it possible I might've actually helped create a new scent?"

"Not a chance!" Clutching her stomach in laughter, Chrissy shook her head. "But you *have* helped me with so much more than that, so thank you."

"Happy to be of help. Anything you need, just ask."

"Well, right now, I need you to clock in so we can open up the shop and actually make some money."

"I'm on it!" Everleigh lifted her hand to her forehead in a salute. "Gotta bring in the big bucks so we can bid our little hearts out tonight. If I win the candy cane wreath, I plan to eat at least half of it tonight!"

"And I'll plan to find someone to cover your shift tomorrow since you'll be sick in bed," Chrissy retorted. "Maybe I should call Nita up and give her advanced warning."

"You're welcome to call Nita, but you can't get rid of

me that easily, sis." Everleigh winked. "You're stuck with me for life."

"Promise?"

"Promise."

There was no doubt in Chrissy's mind it was a promise her sister would forever keep.

NICK

❄

"SIX O'CLOCK ON the dot, Nick, and not a minute after," Grace McHenry instructed with a waggle of her finger in front of her son's face. "I don't want to be late again this year. Last year your father made me wait until the store closed up before we could go. Missed all the bidding wars and we were stuck with a pathetic tinsel eyesore. Looked like something out of *A Charlie Brown Christmas.*"

"I liked that wreath," Joe McHenry called out to his wife from behind the cash register. He looked across the store as he reconciled the till, flipping through a thick stack of ones from the day's transactions. "It had character."

"It certainly had something, but the person who made it had very little in the way of taste," Grace countered. "I've got my eye on Marcia Purcell's this year. That woman has style and her wreath shows it. It's just stunning and will go perfectly on our porch. In fact, I've already bought the matching garland I want to drape over the doorframe right above it. We'll have the best looking door in Heirloom Point, no question about that!"

"Is that the goal? To have the best front door?" Joe asked. He shut the cash register drawer. "I had no idea this was a competition."

"That's exactly what it is!" Grace exclaimed, her tone flabbergasted. "Where have you been?"

"And just what happens when you're outbid on this stylish and stunning wreath, dear?"

"Then I'll bid again and again until I win it."

"Is there a limit?" Nick asked. "You must have a limit, Mom."

He'd never quite understand the rush of excitement she experienced over purchasing a handmade wreath created by one of her neighbors.

"I'll stop when I'm the highest bidder," Grace said. "And not a penny before that!"

Joe lifted his shoulders to his ears and shrugged. "Happy wife, happy life," he justified to his son.

"*Happy wife, empty bank account* sounds more accurate."

"You'll understand when you have a wife of your own," Grace said, only realizing her blunder after the words exited her mouth. Eyes rounded, she offered a meek, "I'm so sorry, Nick. That was insensitive of me."

"No apologies, Mom. We don't do that, remember?"

"I know. I just forget sometimes. I mean, not about the two of you, but..." Her voice wavered. "You know."

"I know." Nick dropped his hands onto his mother's

shoulders and squeezed reassuringly. "I'll be back at six to pick you up."

"On the dot."

"Yes. On the dot."

He had his shoulder against the store's entrance door, readying to go when it suddenly gave way and he nearly fell onto the sidewalk. Luckily, he caught himself at the last minute before his body collided with the pavement.

"Nick McHenry!" A pint-sized woman shouted, her volume almost knocking him down, officially this time. "So the rumors are true—you're actually back!"

Grabbing onto his face, Doris Beasley rotated it side to side in her hands as she peered up at Nick with scrutiny. Then she took his cheek in her thumb and index finger and pinched it the way his Aunt Faith always did when she would visit during birthdays and holidays. He was certain it left a mark.

Nick smiled. "How have you been, Doris?" he asked once her examination was complete. He leaned in for a hug. "How's Earl doing these days?"

"Oh, Earl's fine. Becomes more and more useless as the days go by, though, I tell you. I've asked him to get the Christmas tree down from the attic for two weeks now, but you know how his arthritis flares up with the cold. Now that we've got a big storm coming in, I'll be lucky to have a tree up by Easter!"

"Nick can help you with that," Grace offered, edging her way into the conversation. She had a knack for making any and all business her own. "He'd be happy to. Wouldn't you, Nick?"

Doris's sprite-like face lit up. "Oh, would you, Nick? It would be my very own Christmas miracle if you could!"

It wasn't a request he could say no to, especially not after his mother had offered up his services without asking. While he'd be happy to help Doris out, the thought of scaling a ladder with his knee in its current condition made his stomach roll. Still, he figured between he and Earl, the two could manage just fine.

"I can come by tomorrow morning if that works for you."

Placing her hands on his jaw once again, Doris patted his cheek. "That would be wonderful. You're a good boy, Nick. I've always thought so. Just wish things with you and Chrissy would've worked out. You two were pretty adorable together."

That was Nick's cue to leave. He was happy to help with odd chores around Heirloom Point, but once his past turned into idle chatter and town gossip, he knew it was time to duck out of the conversation.

"Will we see you at the silent auction tonight?" Doris asked.

"Yes, you will," Grace answered for her son once again. It was as though Nick was the puppet and she, the ventriloquist. "He's picking me up at six o'clock." Pinning him with a stare only a mother could get away with, she reiterated, "On the dot."

"Yes, I know, Mom. On the dot. I'll be there."

❄

"IT'S 6:01." GRACE wore an exaggerated frown as she grabbed onto the handle to hoist herself up and into the passenger seat of Nick's truck.

Flashing the face of his phone toward his mother, Nick assured, "Six o'clock on the nose, Mom."

"My watch says one minute after."

"Right, but you manually set your watch. These things automatically set themselves."

She huffed indignantly, a hot breath sputtering between her lips like a horse's nicker. "I don't trust that. Who sets *that* time? A robot? Sounds *real* trustworthy. I've been wearing this watch for nearly a decade and it's never let me down." Grace clicked the seatbelt across her lap. "But we don't have time to argue over timepieces, we have an auction to get to!"

It was a quick drive from the hardware store to the community center. Immediately, Nick recognized several vehicles in the lot that belonged to old buddies from school or to family friends. He hadn't accounted for the night to be a reunion of sorts, but he should've known it had the potential to be one. Heirloom Point was a quaint, close-knit community where people tended to stick around.

"That spot right over there," Grace co-piloted, flapping her hand toward an open parking space near the entrance of the brick building.

Angling the truck into the spot, Nick shut off the engine and pulled in a deep breath.

"You coming?" his mother asked, her purse slung over her shoulder and the truck door cracked open, letting the chilly December air slip into the cab. "We're already five minutes late."

"I'll meet you in there." He forced a grin in an effort to disguise his rising nerves, but his mom knew better. She always did.

"It'll be fine, Nick. I'm sure she'll be happy to see you."

Nick wouldn't go that far. The most he hoped was that it wasn't a total train wreck.

"Go on in, Mom. You don't want Doris outbidding you on that wreath you've had your sights on."

Grace's eyes widened. "You're right! Sure, she's a good deal older than me, but she's got the same taste as I do, doesn't she? Which means she's likely my greatest competition!"

Nick watched as his mom closed the cab door and scurried toward the community center. Several more ladies scampered up the walkway, and he could've been mistaken, but he'd bet money he saw his mom throw an elbow as a cluster of women attempted to squeeze through the sliding automatic doors in front of her, like mice vying for the same piece of cheese. He couldn't help but chuckle at the scene.

He was still laughing when his gaze averted. There, alongside her younger sister, Everleigh, was Chrissy Davenport, trailing up the footpath toward the auction house doors, right behind the frenzied crowd of older women. The sisters hung back, allowing the frantic ladies their space to duke it out like they were rushing toward a Black Friday sale on cutlery. He saw Chrissy's narrow shoulders lift up and drop down in laughter and he figured she found his mother's behavior equally outrageous. Oddly, it felt like a shared moment, and even within the confines of his truck, Nick suddenly felt closer to Chrissy than he had in years. He supposed the physical proximity had a little something to do with that, but he found a reassuring and welcome comfort in the notion that they still found the same things entertaining.

Or maybe he was grasping for a connection that truly wasn't there.

Right before he pulled his gaze from their direction, Everleigh glanced briefly over her shoulder, locking eyes with Nick through the frosted truck windshield. There was nowhere to go, nothing to hide behind or disguise the very real fact that he'd been spotted. Lifting his hand hesitantly, Nick offered a small, guarded wave.

Everleigh acknowledged him with the slightest lift of her nose, then quickly turned toward her sister, ushering her into the building without turning back again.

If Nick had contemplated skipping out on the auction, that was no longer a viable option, not now that he'd been seen. Surely Everleigh would tell Chrissy he was there. He'd look like a complete fool if he darted now.

Steeling himself, he clicked open the driver's side door. Before he even had a boot on the pavement below, a massive hand clasped onto his shoulder, halting him in his tracks.

"Moose McHenry!" a gravely voice bellowed at his back, familiar in tone even if a few octaves lower than the one from his memories. "If Moose hasn't wandered his way back into town!"

"Tucker." Nick spun around to acknowledge his oldest childhood friend. "How on earth have you been, man?"

"*Where* on earth have *you* been is a better question." Stepping back to give Nick a thorough once over, Tucker said, "Oh, that's right. Off making the big bucks with the Lights!"

"Hardly." Nick laughed.

Glancing at Nick's weathered pickup next to them, Tucker narrowed his eyes. "Alright. I believe you on that. This the same junker you had when you got your license?" Tucker kicked the front tire. "Couldn't even afford a new ride? What did they pay you with in Newcastle? Monopoly money?"

"Might as well have been," Nick said. "If you're looking for a get rich quick venture, I don't recommend injured professional hockey player. Especially if you take an entire season off. That kind of kills your paycheck."

"Can't say I'm glad for the injury, but I am glad it landed you back in our neck of the woods. It's been too long, Moose. Too long."

The two stepped up onto the curb, making their way to the auction. Tucker Hayes looked mostly the same, the boyish youth now gone from his cheeks and face, but the same jovial expression present. He was similar in height to Nick—just over six feet tall—and the red hair he'd sported just below his ears in high school was now trimmed neatly above them. And, impressively, he'd finally grown the scruff on his jawline that they'd so often grumbled was an impossible feat back during their teenage years. It was strange to see someone Nick had known since kindergarten now as a grown man, but time had a way of doing that—forcing everyone to grow up.

Nick didn't feel any more grown up, though, as he and Tucker neared the entrance. In fact, the same butterflies that swarmed in his stomach the first time he'd asked Chrissy to dance at the Fall Formal had taken flight again. Nick was all clammy hands, perspiration laden brow, and queasy, worried stomach. He was in worse shape than the night of his debut with the Northern Lights, and he'd gotten sick in a trash can before taking to the ice then. If his past was any indicator, tonight would end in a similar manner.

"You here to bid on a wreath?" Tucker asked as the two pressed into the crowd gathered just inside the door. A line two dozen people deep stretched out from a folding table near the front where attendees awaited the assignment of their bidding number.

"I suppose so. Mostly my mom needed a ride, so I thought I'd scope things out."

"Scope things out, or scope *someone* out?"

It would've frustrated Nick that this was everyone's first assumption had it not been blatantly true. The community center was the perfect neutral ground for a first interaction. It was Switzerland. Of course he'd thought about stopping into Chrissy's candle shop, but on her home turf, Nick didn't know what to expect. And had she wandered her way into his parents' store, they'd have more than a few spectators in the peanut gallery of public opinion. The *Silent Night Silent Auction* created an ideal crowd to get lost in.

And at the moment, that's exactly what Chrissy had done.

Nick straightened his spine to peer over the tops of heads, but he couldn't locate her.

"Numbers seventy-two and seventy-three." A woman he recognized as Miss Sandra, the local high school nurse, scribbled the numbers onto separate index cards with a thick, black marker. "Bidding closes at 8:00 p.m. sharp, so be sure to keep an eye on your final bids and close out no later than 8:30." She looked up as she slid the notecards across the table to the men. "Nick McHenry!" she roared suddenly, dropping her pen and bounding to her feet. Yanking Nick over the table, she drew him into a giant hug. "I heard you were coming home but didn't believe it could be true! The return of a hometown hero!"

"My brother's the real hero in our family, ma'am," Nick noted, knowing his older brother's service to their country was the only status worthy of true heroism. To get any sort of recognition for mere entertainment when Kevin was off securing their freedom felt ill-placed. "I'm just a mediocre hockey player."

"You're more than that, Nick. Oh goodness. Just look at you!" Sandra squealed. She jumped up and down on the balls of her feet. "Handsome as ever, I must say! You always were such a good looking young man."

Nick peeled himself from her arms that clung with boa constrictor-like force.

"Good to see you again, Miss Sandra. None of the physical therapists or doctors that worked on me over the years ever offered lollipops like you always did. Made me almost long for the high school injuries that landed me in your office every other week."

"You know, I still give those out. Sugar free now since the school's passed some healthy eating initiative, but stop by sometime and I'll make sure you get your proper fix. Just bought a new bag."

"Will do," Nick said with a chuckle. He picked up his bidding number, placed it in his jacket pocket, and followed Tucker into the auditorium. What often served as a gym equipped with basketball hoops and retractable stands now displayed over a hundred holiday wreaths, all hung on the walls around the court like a museum made of Christmas cheer. On the table directly underneath each wreath was a sheet of lined paper, ready to be filled with the back and forth of bids of friendly—and not-so-friendly—competition.

"Remember the year we bid on behalf of Prosper Tomlin? Junior year, I think. Didn't he end up taking home about a dozen or more wreaths by the time the night was over?" Tucker reminisced as he looked around the packed space. He tipped his head in cordial greeting to each neighbor that walked by while they moved about the room. "Think he hung one on each of his horse stalls, if I remember correctly. Had to use them somehow, I suppose."

"You say 'on behalf' like we were doing him a favor, Tuck. I'm fairly certain he's the one that called the cops on me and Chrissy that night on his pond. Some sort of wreath revenge."

"You know, he doesn't even come to these anymore," Tucker said around a guilty laugh. "Think we effectively ruined it for him?"

"I think we ruined a lot of things back in our day. The time the brakes went out on your dad's 1967 Mustang and we jumped the curb at over forty miles an hour. Mr. Kelleher's garage window when I hit that grand slam the summer of our sixth grade year." Nick lifted a finger with each recollection, ticking them off one by one. "The drama class's performance of *A Midsummer Night's Dream*—popcorn disaster of the century. Senior prom with the faulty smoke machine. Graduation and the gown mishap. The list could—and does—go on."

"Rather than ruining, I like to think we took each of those things to an entirely new level. Really left our mark on them." Squeezing his buddy's shoulder, Tucker said, "We sure had some good times together, didn't we, Moose?"

"The best."

And they did. Growing up in Heirloom Point with a friend like Tucker Hayes made for an unforgettable upbringing. Nick knew it was a rare and treasured gift to have a friendship like that—one he could pick up right where he left off, as though the years crossed off the calendar were nothing more than a miniscule blip in the landscape of time. They'd kept in touch over the last decade, mostly following one another on various social medias, liking posts where appropriate and texting for birthdays. It was all surface conversation, but there was a satisfying security found in the fact that all of those small correspondences strung together to maintain a friendship.

Nick's chest tightened with the far off hope that it could be the same with Chrissy, as well, even though their communication had been altogether nonexistent. He knew the odds were against him when it came to that particular Christmas wish.

"Look at this, Moose!" Tucker's already booming voice lifted in volume. He rushed forward, grabbing a wreath from its hook and shoving it into Nick's chest. "You have to bid on this! It couldn't be more perfect."

"Is it actually a moose?" Nick asked, holding the wreath out in examination. "Looks like it could be a reindeer."

"No, it's definitely a moose."

The sound of the voice at his back made his mouth go dry, his jaw clamp down in tension.

"I still can't believe you let him call you that for all those years," she said, coming up alongside him. "Hi, Nick." Chrissy Davenport beamed her brilliant smile, the one that lit up her face, along with the entire room. "It's been a long time."

CHRISSY

TIME DID LITTLE to change his appearance. Sure, his features were more masculine now, his jaw squared and shoulders broader. But he still sported that boyish grin, the one that made her knees turn to jelly when she was on the receiving end of it. It was a smile of intention, not merely obligation.

"Scone at ten o'clock," Everleigh had whispered less than five minutes into the event.

"Don't you mean biscuit?"

Everleigh slapped her forehead. "Right. Yes. Biscuit. This whole code word thing doesn't really work if I can't keep my baked goods straight."

"I don't see him." Chrissy had said, pressing up on her toes to peer above the crowds. She could feel her pulse in her neck and her stomach quivering with nerves, but there was an excitement coursing through her at the possibility of seeing Nick again that she hadn't anticipated.

"Ten o'clock. Or is it two o'clock. I'm not good with clocks." Grabbing her sister's shoulders, Everleigh swiveled Chrissy around. "Over there. See? Next to Tucker Hayes."

It was a scene right out of their high school days, when Nick and Tucker would lean up against their lockers during the passing periods, appearing both casual and intimidating simultaneously. Chrissy could still recall the day she'd finally mustered enough bravery to march over to Nick to introduce herself. She'd plotted for a full week, even going as far as to recite in front of the mirror to make sure she got it just right—not too forced, not too spontaneous. Simply friendly. Her family had been new to Heirloom Point at the time, her father just starting out on the police force. She knew who Nick McHenry was—everyone did—his athleticism creating not only a buzz about town, but instant popularity at school. But Chrissy was the new girl with no reputation, no real reason to stand out in the teenage crowd.

And just like she'd done on that December day as a freshman, she'd gathered her courage and pressed through the mass of people, making determined strides across the auditorium until she stood directly behind the only man to ever hold—and break—her heart.

Chrissy had never felt that heart beating more strongly than in this new moment; it threatened to burst right out of her chest.

She had joined their conversation uninvited, but when she'd uttered his name, the tender expression on Nick's face swallowed up all of those years, making it feel like only yesterday in a way that was so inexplicable, it felt almost magical.

"Chrissy." His caramel-colored eyes met hers, holding her gaze long enough to make her throat go dry. Nick passed the wreath to Tucker, then stuck his hand into the gap between he and Chrissy, offering it for a shake. She couldn't help but feel it seemed too formal for the long history they shared. Even still, Chrissy reached for his proffered hand, but at the last second Nick tugged her into his arms. "It's good to see you," he said close to her ear, his breath startlingly warm on her cheek. "Really good."

"You too, Nick," Chrissy replied as she gently eased out of his embrace. His sandy blond hair was tousled the same way he'd styled it in his youth and even though he wore a tan canvas jacket, Chrissy could see that Nick had maintained his muscular, fit build over the years. So much of him was different, but all the best parts remained the same.

"You look good, Chrissy," Nick iterated the words she had just been thinking.

"You, too," she reciprocated.

"Doesn't look like much of a moose anymore, does he?" Tucker hung the wreath back onto its hook and then jostled Nick with an aggressive shoulder bump.

"That was such an unfortunate nickname." Everleigh frowned. She stepped up to join the conversation. "Who even came up with that awful label?"

"Yours truly." Extending his arms out on either side to stretch to his full wingspan, Tucker plastered on the proudest of smirks. "Remember that big ol' nose and those too-big-for-his-head ears?" He bellowed a haughty laugh, making playful fun of his longtime friend. "Nick was total moose status."

"Oh, right," Everleigh humored. "Because as I recall, you were *so* good looking as a gangly teenager."

"Why else do you think they called me Tuck the Buck? You've seen how handsome an actual buck is, right? People literally display their heads above their fireplaces, just so they can stare at them all day. Compare a moose to that—not even remotely the same. Hanging out with Nick back then made me look like an Adonis!"

"Well isn't it reassuring that some things never change?" Everleigh rolled her eyes and bumped into Tucker's side as she shoved past. "I'd love to stay and help inflate your already bursting ego, but I have a candy cane wreath to claim."

"Did you say candy cane?" Tucker perked up like he was a dog being told it was time to go for a walk. "My all-time favorite Christmas treat!"

"Oh, no you don't." Everleigh's grin instantly flipped into a scowl. Her eyes narrowed into intimidating slits. "That wreath is mine!"

"Or mine." Tucker shrugged. "We shall see who the highest bidder is at the end of the night." Winking, his mouth pulled up just on one side, scheming evident in his eyes. "Plus, we should leave ChrisMoose to themselves. They've got more than a few years to catch up on."

"I completely forgot about *that* nickname, too." Everleigh threw her hands into the air. "Man, you're full of them. I'm surprised you didn't have a nickname for me."

"Oh, he did." Chrissy stifled a laugh. She caught Nick's eye and they exchanged a knowing glance, like they could read each other's thoughts.

"What? What was it?" Prodding, Everleigh's gaze bounced back and forth between the three friends in front of her. "Someone tell me!"

"Off to bid on some peppermint goodness!" Tuck shouted. He used his best hockey moves to dart through the crowd in an agile attempt to outrace Everleigh, who immediately followed after, hot on his trail.

Looking up at Nick, Chrissy smiled, albeit hesitantly. With her sister security blanket gone, the anxiety she experienced in small doses earlier swept in like a northern wind, disorienting her and making her want to run for cover. She swallowed around the lump in her throat. "So, you're back in Heirloom Point for some time?"

"That's the plan." Nick rocked on his heels, his hands deep in the pockets of his jacket. Lifting his shoulders in a shrug, he looked like he was about to say more, but the words didn't follow.

"You and Tucker kept in touch?"

Nick looked over his shoulder, seeking out his friend. "Yeah, a bit. We haven't seen each other in years, but we've communicated on and off."

Chrissy nodded. She couldn't tell if it was jealously coursing through her, or something else entirely, because even if Nick had reached out during the last decade, she wasn't sure she would've been ready for it. She wasn't sure she was ready for it now.

"I bet your parents love having you home."

"Well, I'm not technically *home*-home. Remember Mr. Davies?" Chrissy nodded. He often frequented her shop to buy candles for his classroom. "I'm renting his in-law quarters until I can find a more permanent solution."

"Is that why you're here? To find a wreath now that you actually have a door?" Looking down at her feet, Chrissy laughed under her breath. "I assumed you were back with your parents and thought how funny it would be if you planned to put a wreath on that bedroom door. You'd have to do some serious rearranging, what with all the posters and bumper stickers you had plastered on it back in the day."

"Would you believe they're all still on there? Mom hasn't changed a thing since I left."

"That's actually really comforting"—Chrissy looked up, her gaze colliding with Nick's—"that some things don't change."

"You looking for a wreath for the shop?" He changed the subject and Chrissy wondered if she'd been too forthright, too blunt. She had no idea how to communicate with this new version of the only person she'd ever loved. "I hear you're the most successful small business owner in town. Mom says you've won the Heart of Heirloom Point award three years in a row. Congratulations, Chrissy."

Chrissy's cheeks went hot, unsure how to accept the compliment even though she could sense it was a genuine one. "It's just a silly award the chamber of commerce gives out each year. I think it's rigged, actually. My dad's a board member, so that just screams conflict of interest, but what can I say, Heirloom Point is a very supportive town."

"Don't I know it," Nick agreed. "I could always feel the love, even from two-thousand miles away."

The word *love* made Chrissy's breath catch. Scrambling for something to say to redirect, she stumbled over her words like they were caught in a traffic jam in her mouth. "I think...um...do you know how long the bidding lasts?"

"Eight o'clock, I believe. That's what Miss Sandra told us at registration."

"I should probably look for something to bid on soon, then. I know it gets pretty competitive during that last half hour. It's every man for himself."

Nick chuckled. "Have your eyes on anything in particular?" he asked and she couldn't tell if he really cared to know the answer, or if he was just making polite small talk. Their conversation had turned that direction.

"Actually, I sort of do this thing where I bid on the ones that don't have any bids at all at the end of the night. I mean, I always feel bad that some wreaths have these massive bidding wars, while others go completely unnoticed. I usually end up with a few for that reason, but the shop has ample space to display them, so I don't mind at all."

"And that right there is why you keep getting the Heart of Heirloom Point award."

"Because I buy a lot of wreaths?" She laughed. "I guess technically I am pouring back into the community—"

"No, it's because you have such a heart for this town and all of the people in it. Sort of makes you the heart of it all."

If Chrissy hadn't known how to read any of Nick's earlier compliments, this one felt like it had been spoken in an entirely different language. The translation eluded her. Hooking her thumb over her shoulder, she said, "I should go look around to see what's left." Then she paused before adding, "Would you like to come with me?"

"I would, but I've left my mom unattended for far too long now. I can't even imagine all of the trouble she's likely gotten herself into while unsupervised." Touching Chrissy's elbow lightly, he said, "It was really good to see you again, Chrissy."

"You too, Nick."

Good was one word to describe it. But there were many others that tangled together in Chrissy's heart, descriptors for every range of emotion. Backing away, she swiveled on the heel of her boot and scanned the crowd for her sister. Holiday music rang out through the auditorium speakers, the jingle of classic carols filling the community center as the soundtrack of the season. A percussion of chatter created an energetic buzz in sync with the music, and it made it impossible not to feel as though Christmas had already arrived. This tradition was the big kick off to the holiday and everyone knew it, their participation in the *Silent Night Silent Auction* a heart-warming way to usher in the season.

A momentary panic fell over Chrissy, her unfinished candle scent hanging over her like homework. She knew she couldn't force it. She'd done that before and even though no one knew, those candles never sold quite as well as the ones she poured all of her heart and soul into, right along with the fragrance and wax.

Nick's mention of Chrissy's heart for the community had thrown her. It was a nice thing to say, but given he hadn't been a part of the community for ten years, he had little authority in saying it.

The further removed from Nick's proximity and their conversation, the less Chrissy felt held under his spell. Seeing Nick had done something to Chrissy and she instantly reverted back to that doe-eyed school girl. The questions she'd wanted to ask—the ones she'd played over and over like a track on repeat—flitted right out of her head. She didn't think he had tried to charm her intentionally, it just happened. It always just happened with Nick McHenry.

"Everleigh!" Chrissy blurted as soon as she caught sight of her sister across the room. There, staking her claim next to a candy cane gilded wreath, was Everleigh, pen in her white-knuckled grip.

"Hey, sis." She offered half of her attention to Chrissy while the other half scanned the room, keeping a watchful eye out for anyone who might come between her and the coveted peppermint wreath. "Sorry I kinda left you there, but"—she waved a hand over the wreath —"priorities, right? How'd it go with Nick?"

"It was fine." Chrissy hesitated. "I think."

Stepping forward with her pen readied, Everleigh lingered while a middle-aged woman walked up to the table and jotted her bid and number onto a blank line. Once the woman angled to walk away, Everleigh scribbled something onto the sheet underneath her bid, a massive grin on her face, like she'd just pulled a fast one. "Just fine? Not monumental? Life changing? Destiny altering?"

"No, definitely none of those things. I don't know. It was comfortable. Like an old sweater, you know? Familiar and cozy."

"Um, no, I don't know. Nick McHenry is no old sweater, Chris. Did you *see* him? He looks fantastic."

Chrissy wasn't about to admit out loud that she absolutely agreed. "It just felt a little *too* comfortable, though, you know? Like we could so easily slip right back into the way things were without even talking about what happened."

"Do I sense the revival of ChrisMoose on the horizon?"

"That was the cheesiest relationship name ever."

"Well, of course it was. Tucker made it up. What would you expect?"

"Speaking of, where is he?"

Everleigh shrugged nonchalantly. "I figure he's gone into stealth mode. Probably off somewhere spying on me and this wreath, just waiting to swoop in at the last second and steal all of my candy cane dreams."

"I think he'd like to swoop in and steal a little more than that from you, Ev."

Her sister's face went blank. "What are you talking about?"

"Seriously? You can't be that clueless."

Everleigh's expression remained void of any comprehension, the ultimate deer caught in the disorienting headlight glow.

"He always had the biggest crush on you, sis. Called you *Meant For Me Everleigh.* You're telling me you had no idea? I thought everyone knew; it was pretty obvious."

"Um, no, I certainly did not know. I mean, the guy does think awful highly of himself now, but I totally would've dated him in my younger years had he just asked me out." Grinning coyly, she said, "Dated him, maybe, but let him steal this incredible, edible wreath from me? Not a chance!"

Everleigh switched back into alert mode, her only mission to secure ownership of the candied wreath at her side. Even though she wanted to talk more about her encounter with Nick, Chrissy knew she'd have to wait until later to have her sister's ear. Everleigh was like a cat, not one with the gift of multi-tasking.

"I'm going to go look around."

"Sure thing." Preoccupied, Everleigh's eyes darted about the room.

"I'll find you at close out."

"Yep!" Answering now only in one word sentences,

Chrissy had lost any bit of what little attention her sister had left to give.

While it was obvious certain wreaths drew more consideration than others, Chrissy was pleased with the overall buzz at the event. The energy was palpable. In fact, she had a hard time locating any wreaths that didn't already have at least one bid, the competitive spirit high and bids even higher. That fact made her burst with small town pride.

After completing two full laps around the room just to be sure she hadn't missed anything, Chrissy scribbled her number onto the paper below an ordinary, run-of-the-mill wreath that looked like it could be purchased from the holiday section of any department store. It wasn't ugly at all, there just wasn't anything special about it to make it stand out. Even still, Chrissy felt an obligation to offer her bid. If she didn't, it risked being the only wreath to go unclaimed. Even if the wreath was nothing special, Chrissy figured the person who made it had to be. That someone took time out of their schedule to create something to bring in money for charity was a special thing. While the wreath was lackluster, Chrissy doubted the person was.

By the end of the night, she'd consumed half a dozen sugar cookies, made pleasant chatter with her friends and storefront neighbors, and successfully avoided another run in with Nick. Every time she'd spotted him, she'd ducked away, thankful for the crowd to take cover in. One conversation for the evening felt plenty sufficient.

As Miss Sandra came over the speakers at final call,

urging all participants to make their last bids, the activity in the room kicked into high gear. Women decked in knit Christmas sweaters shoved about; husbands scooted out of the way to avoid an altercation. Chrissy figured her father was busy standing his post, this portion of the night the most potential for a ruckus. Chrissy could hear Everleigh shout something along the lines of "Candy time, it's all mine!" and she knew she would head home with either an extremely elated, or extremely dejected, sister. She prayed for the former.

Tossing her empty hot chocolate cup into a nearby trash can, Chrissy made her way to the only wreath she'd bid on all night. Looking at the sheet, she saw she had remained the single bid throughout the evening, no one else wishing to hang this particularly plain wreath on their door.

"Their loss," Chrissy muttered to herself as she pulled the paper from the table and wreath from the wall. It wasn't the best looking wreath, but the spirit in which it had been created and purchased was enough to make Chrissy proud to hang it on her shop door the very next morning. For her, it was just perfect.

NICK

❄

NICK GRABBED HIS jacket from the hook next to the door and stepped out onto the front stoop. The morning air met him with an icy embrace. Shivering, he reached back to snag his scarf before locking up the house. He wrapped the fabric around his neck in two loops and then buried his hands in his pockets, quickening his pace to stride up the drive and onto the sidewalk.

The Beasley home was a short distance from his rental. Doris was eager for help with the tree, as she'd already called him twice that morning to confirm. It was barely nine. It would be good to check the task off of Nick's list, though he didn't mind helping his neighbors. He often thought back to the time Earl gave his truck a jumpstart when he had been a new driver and didn't know not to leave the radio running when the engine wasn't. Nick had stranded himself in front of their downtown coffee shop, *Jitters*, and Earl quickly came to his rescue, jumper cables in hand, smile on his kind face.

Though he knew the gesture didn't require repayment, it would be good to reciprocate the favor, even if a dozen years after the fact.

Puffing out a breath that suspended in front of his face for a moment before it dispersed, Nick tried not to inhale too deeply. The air was stinging cold and his lungs tightened with each frosty breath. Wishing his bum knee would allow a faster pace, Nick pressed forward, eager for the warm escape the Beasley home promised.

He had to check his phone for the house number, failing to remember which one belonged to the couple. One house he did recognize, however, was Lee Davenport's, just three homes south of the Beasley address. A pair of empty rocking chairs were perched on the front porch, just like they had been the last time he visited. The last conversation Nick had with Lee took place in those chairs. Nick hadn't intentionally rocked in his, but his nerves had trembled out of his body, making the rocking inevitable. It felt the same as pacing back and forth, that anxious, uncontrollable habit.

Nick never imagined Lee would grant permission for Chrissy's hand. They were young—newly turned twenty —and the idea of a father gladly giving away his daughter in marriage to a man without a steady income or real job wasn't a favorable one.

But not only had Lee agreed to give Nick his blessing, he'd been happy to do so.

"I'll finally have the son I've always wanted," Lee had

said, a comment that Nick felt so deep inside that it became a part of him. Whether intentional or not, he'd wanted to live a life that made Lee proud, something in him craving that approval from the man he greatly admired.

To that very day, Nick hadn't been able to shake the shock of Lee's blessing. And he hadn't been able to muster up the courage to speak to him after everything had unraveled.

Nick had been nervous to see Chrissy again, but he'd been terrified to encounter her father. He was glad that meeting had yet to occur.

Ambling up the pathway, Nick arrived at the Beasley home in good time. He lifted his hand to knock —just below an ornate wreath he assumed had been purchased at the auction—when the door swung open before his fist could meet the solid wood. His hand hung in the air.

"Good morning, Nick! Or is it even still considered morning?" Doris flipped her wrist over, a trio of bangle bracelets clanging together. Her eyes squinted as she examined her watch.

"I apologize, ma'am," Nick began as Doris waved him into the foyer and motioned for his scarf and jacket. "I slept in a bit today."

"I suppose that's allowed," the petite woman teased. "And as I remember, that was the precise reason you only lasted two days at the coffee shop. Kept oversleeping."

"I made it three days, I think. Never even got a chance to learn the espresso machine, though," Nick corrected with a wide grin. "But you're right; I do enjoy my sleep."

Nodding in the direction of her husband, who reclined in a leather chair in the living room just off the entryway, Doris said, "So does Earl."

The man gargled a perfectly timed snore.

"Earl!" Doris barked. "Get up! Nick is here to help with the tree."

Snapping into an upright position, Earl launched from his chair. "Who's there?" He whipped his head back and forth and then fumbled for his glasses on the side table. Once fitted to his face, his worried expression relaxed and he grinned as the young visitor came into focus. "Well, if it isn't Nick McHenry? Good to see you!"

"Same to you." Nick went in for a handshake, but his knee buckled underneath him and he had to grab onto the back of the sofa to keep from tumbling to the ground. All pride rushed out in that instant, the look of shocked pity in both Doris and Earl's eyes enough to make him feel small.

"Careful, Nick," Doris quipped. "If you injure yourself again, then I'm really not going to have a tree to put out at all this year. Be a gentleman and wait until after it's down from the attic before you go hurting yourself, please." She winked.

"Yes, ma'am." Nick smiled, grateful in that moment of embarrassment for a bit of levity.

Doris grabbed his elbow. "Let's go. The attic access is in the back hall. I've already got out the ladder, I just need you to go up and get the tree."

Following his instruction, Nick trailed behind Doris, Earl shuffling a few feet back. Doris was a dynamo, her energy level unmatched not only in her own age group, but likely among everyone else in town. She was quick witted and spirited, her reaction giving Nick little opportunity to feel sorry for himself, and for that, he was thankful.

Taking to the ladder, Nick gripped the sides firmly with his hands, hoping his knee didn't pull another stunt like it had back in the living room.

"Just give the hatch a good whack. It sticks a bit."

Nick did as instructed. The attic trapdoor creaked open, dust particles releasing into the air. Stifling a cough, Nick budged it open all the way.

"We're in!"

Using all of his upper body strength, he hoisted himself into the crawl space. Immediately, he was met with thick, stale air. Years' worth of memories stored in the dank attic filtered out in a musty, wafting aroma. While the Beasley's kept their home tidied and presentable, the attic was a free for all, boxes littered about the cramped interior like the sorting room of a post office.

"Any clue where it might be?" Nick hollered down through the ceiling opening.

"Earl?" Doris yelled. "Where'd you put the tree last year?"

"Well, I don't know, Dory. Somewhere in the attic. Next to a bunch of old boxes, I think."

"A bunch of old boxes," Nick muttered, chuckling. It

was a fair assessment that the amount of old boxes was incalculable. "You have any idea which old boxes? West wall or east wall?"

"Gosh. You know—I don't actually remember," Earl said taking to the first rung of the ladder to peer up into the attic. "Maybe the south?"

"Earl doesn't even remember what he ate for breakfast this morning," Doris said. "I said it before, but it will be an honest to goodness Christmas miracle if I get my tree up at all this year."

"We'll get your tree up, Doris. I just need to look around a bit."

In truth, it would take more than a bit. Nick figured he'd need a good hour to locate anything in the disorganized attic. Pulling his phone from his back pocket, he swept up on the screen to illuminate the flashlight. It didn't help much, but he could now see his feet and make a pathway through the packages so as not to stumble about.

Sweeping the ray of light back and forth, Nick read the labels on the boxes, locating every possible holiday except Christmas. Then, peeking out just above a stack of milk crates, he spotted a green, leafy branch.

"Think I might've found something!" Nick called out. Yanking on the object, he tugged it free, dejected when it pulled out too easily. "Never mind. Just a wreath," he said, but his choice of wording wasn't accurate at all. It wasn't *just* a wreath, it was a beautiful one, definitely more impressive than any of the wreaths he saw the night before at the auction. Blowing onto it, dust flickered into the air like bits of stardust illuminated in the stream of light from his phone.

"You might want to put this out on display, Doris." Nick crouched down to pass the wreath to Earl through the open hatch. "It's too pretty to keep tucked away in an attic."

"Would you look at that?" Doris's voice became thick with emotion. "Earl, remember this?"

"Absolutely," her husband said, his tone equally filled with awe. "I don't have as bad a memory as you think, my dear." He winked at his wife, giving her shoulder a squeeze. "And I had maple raisin oatmeal for breakfast. See? Sharp as a tack."

Dropping his legs down, Nick placed his feet on the top of the ladder. "I honestly don't see the tree up here, Doris. I'm sorry."

"It's okay, Nick. I'll just go without this year," Doris said, unreasonably dejected. "No Christmas miracle for me."

"Now that I think of it, didn't we leave it on the street during curb pickup last spring?" Earl asked. "Remember? All the strands but one were out and last Christmas you said you couldn't stand to look at the sorry excuse for a tree for one more season. Something about getting rid of it since it no longer brought you joy. See? I *do* remember things, dear."

A sheepish grin spread onto Doris's lips. "Well, that doesn't sound right," she countered, unwilling to give in.

"No," Earl pressed. "I remember it clear as day now. We had it out there right next to the shattered Easter platter. I commented how ironic it was that we were getting rid of both a Christmas tree and an Easter decoration. Thought our friends from church might start to worry about us."

The more her husband continued, the more Doris's mouth turned downward. "Alright, alright. We don't have a tree. I'm sorry to have wasted your time, Nick, but I do appreciate you coming by."

"It wasn't a waste of time. I found the wreath, at least," he said, carefully descending the ladder. "Maybe you could put that up for now?"

"I've already got one on our door that nearly cost me a kidney. What about you? Did you bid on one last night?"

"No, ma'am," he answered. "That's alright, though. My parents are selling a few at the store. I can always snag one of those."

Shoving the wreath into Nick's chest, Doris said, "Take this one, dear. It has far too much value to be crammed away in a dusty attic. We'd love for you to have it."

Nick agreed. A wreath of that caliber deserved to be on display for all to see.

"Accept it as my payment for officially wasting your morning. I'm just so embarrassed."

"No need to be. Wasn't a waste at all." Nick followed the couple through the house and to the front door where he collected his scarf and coat, readying to leave. "You know, Tucker's family tree lot opens up this weekend. Maybe a real Christmas tree is in order for this year?"

"I like that idea, Nick. We always put up the fake one out of convenience, but I do miss that crisp pine scent of a freshly cut tree. Might take your suggestion on that."

Nick tipped his head as he said his goodbyes and headed back toward his rented house, new wreath in hand. It wasn't that it was intricately decorated, but something about it brought a warmth to Nick's chest that no jacket could. Flipping it over, he noticed a small, white tag and when he read the name neatly written on it perfect cursive, his heart caught on a beat.

❄

THE PLAN WAS to hang the wreath and then run. Well, hobble, more accurately, since running wasn't on the list of things Nick was very skilled at anymore. To his relief, a long nail stuck out of the door, almost as though it was awaiting the wreath's return, like a porch light left on by a parent after curfew. Nick lifted the decoration quietly, breath secured in his lungs, footsteps kept purposefully light. His entire body sagged with relief once the wreath was lowered onto the nail. Backing away, Nick swiveled on his heel to go.

The lock turned over.

"Nick?"

Eyes shut, Nick's composure slumped further. "Mr. Davenport. Sir."

"How are you, son?" Chrissy's father glanced around, scanning his surroundings like he was on patrol. "Is everything okay?"

"Yes, sir. I just—" Nick racked his brain to form an excuse, but his thoughts didn't come fast enough.

The pallor of Lee's face drained of all pigment as his gaze swung back toward his front door. "Did you...?" His voice trailed off. He pointed to the wreath as his brow creased in confusion.

"I found it in the Beasley's attic. Didn't realize who it belonged to until I saw the nametag on the back. I'm sorry if I've overstepped by bringing it here, sir. I just figured it was something you might like to have back."

"No." Lee paused. His eyes remained fixed on the wreath when he answered, "You haven't overstepped, Nick. Not at all."

Nick figured the words were meant as a comfort, but the strained look on Lee's face made him question whether he had done the right thing. Regret took root in his gut.

"Nick, would you like to come in for a cup of coffee?" Lee's gaze clung to the wreath, studying it, examining every minute detail. He shook his head, tossing off the stare as he angled toward Nick. "I'd love to catch up if you have a moment."

Nick did have ample time to spare, his only plan to stop by the hardware store later in the day to help his dad with a delivery of space heaters.

"Of course, sir." Nick rubbed his hands together, creating the friction necessary for warmth. "That would be great."

"Having a real cold snap around these parts." Lee pushed the door open with his hand and motioned for

Nick to go on ahead. As though he was entirely mystified by the wreath, he stole another brief look before shutting the door. "Everleigh just got me a new espresso machine for my birthday and I figure I should test it out. Care to be the guinea pig?"

Nick laughed. "There's one of those fancy things at my place, too."

"Really?" Lee perked up. "Maybe you could give me a few pointers?"

"I've yet to use it. That thing intimidates me and I even worked at a coffee shop once!"

"It intimidates me, too. I restored my dad's '57 Chevy, but a dang coffee maker has me feeling like a real dummy. Glad to know I'm not the only one. I told Everleigh I was just fine with my old coffee pot, but she insisted I needed to join the twenty-first century. Apparently that means drinking frou-frou coffee drinks."

"I won't lie. They can be pretty good. Almost like a dessert."

"I'm always up for dessert," Lee said. Their conversation was a surface one, no arguing that, but there was a comfort in it, merely because there was comfort in being in the Davenport home again.

For years, it had been a home away from home for Nick, so much so that sometimes he even failed to knock before entering. In those days, Lee had given him a hard time about that—that although Nick was like family, there were still boundaries to adhere to.

Nick couldn't shove down the feeling that showing

up unannounced with the wreath was one boundary he'd grossly overstepped.

Lee stared at the shiny espresso machine on the counter, his face scrunched, his mustache curving above his lip. "I don't know, Nick." He smacked a hand on the counter. "This might be above my skillset. You okay with some tea instead?"

"Yes, sir. That would be just fine."

Lee nodded, appearing thankful for the flexibility. He pulled a teapot from the stove and turned on the tap to fill it with water before returning it to the burner. Taking two mugs down from the cupboard, he placed one on the kitchen table and held the other in his large hand. Nick lowered into the nearby chair.

"I was sorry to hear about your injury, Nick." Lee paused, correcting, he said, "Well, *see* your injury, I suppose. And hear it, too." He cringed. "That was pretty hard to watch, son."

"It was pretty hard to experience," Nick replied. "And hard to watch, I'm sure. I'll give you that. I think it replayed a few dozen times on national television. I lost track."

"It was a slow news day that day," Lee offered with a chuckle. "How is it now?"

Inadvertently, Nick rubbed at his knee, something he did more often than not. "It still bugs me on and off, but it's fine."

"And do you think you'll ever get out on the ice again?"

"In a professional capacity?" Nick asked. "No, sir, I doubt that."

"Recreationally, then?"

"It's possible, but if I'm completely honest, it's more of a struggle than I care to admit just to walk on solid ground some days. The thought of having only ice underneath me is a bit terrifying."

Lee's face fell. "I'm sorry to hear that. Truly."

"It's alright. It was a great ride while it lasted, so I suppose it was worth it all in the end."

"I hope it was."

Nick doubted the tone of Lee's statement was meant to be accusatory in nature, but he sensed it, woven into the words. Before he could answer, the teapot whistled like a screeching owl.

Lee grabbed the handle, poured the steaming hot water into Nick's mug, and offered a small wire basket with various flavors of tea bags. Nick chose an orange mint and dropped it into the mug to steep.

"I must be completely honest, Nick—I was awfully surprised to see that wreath on my door. Even more surprised to see you on the other side of it."

"I'm sorry, sir—"

"No apologies necessary. It was a really nice thing to do. Didn't figure anyone hung onto her stuff over the years, you know? I've kept so many of her things, but I've had to part with some things, too. This wreath was a nice surprise."

Nick blew across the top of his mug to cool the contents. Words failed him in the moment. "I'm sorry—"

He had to force a swallow around the ball forming in his throat. "I'm sorry I didn't make it out for her service, sir."

Lee waved him off. He pulled in a long sip from his cup, then smoothed his moustache with his fingers. "You weren't even in the country, Nick. We didn't expect you to."

"But I still should've been there. Audrey was like a second mom to me," he said, guilt weighty in his voice and in his heart, too. That heaviness had been a constant over the years. "I should've been there for Chrissy."

Clamping a hand onto Nick's shoulder, Lee left it there, his grip reassuring. "Chrissy was okay, Nick. She got to spend a lot of time with her mom in that final year and when it came down to their goodbyes, they were both ready for it."

Those words didn't console Nick any. He knew he'd let them all down. Before he could offer another apology, Lee interjected, "I'm sure things won't ever go back to the way they were, but I need you to know that I don't hold anything against you, Nick."

"I'm glad to hear it, sir. Do you think Chrissy does?"

"Well, that is something you'll have to ask her."

Nick suspected that would be the answer. The small talk had been easy with Chrissy the night before and surprisingly easier with her father at present, but the deeper conversations—breaking through the ice and delving deep into the murky waters of the past—that would take more time.

And as fate would have it, time was the one thing Nick seemed to have plenty of lately.

CHRISSY

"NITA, YOU'RE GOING to do just great," Chrissy said. "You were made for this job."

"Well, I don't know about that, sweetie, but I can sure try my best. Ever since Carl passed, I've just been spinning my wheels at home. It'll be good to have some real responsibility for a change. Something to force me out of the house, you know?"

"I can understand that." Chrissy had felt a similar, profound loss when her mother died, but for her, coming into the candle shop was cathartic. It was a place of true and restorative healing. She hoped she could create a similar atmosphere for her newly widowed friend. "I just wish it was warmer in here. Ted promised to come by this afternoon, but I don't hold out much hope of him fulfilling that promise. He's given me the same one for over a week now."

"Ted tends to do that," Nita said as she straightened a row of candles on a shelf, lining them up like spices in a cabinet. "Over promise, under deliver." She turned toward her young friend and, as though warming her hands over a fire, held her palms above the small flickering flames of one of Chrissy's three-wick candles. She shivered. "Any chance you have a space heater we can use? I bet that would warm the shop up in no time."

Chrissy knew it would, but she had stubbornly clung to her resolve not to march across the street and purchase one. She could get by just fine with an extra layer of clothing and fashionable scarf coiled around her neck. Her older friend, however, was not prepared for the wintery temperatures inside the store, wearing too few layers to keep adequately comfortable.

"Oh, for goodness sake!" Everleigh blurted the very second she burst through the shop door. Her entrance was typically eccentric and today's was no exception as she threw her hands up wildly, like she was tossing confetti into the air. "Chrissy, this is absolutely ridiculous. I get that you want it to *look* like the North Pole in here, but it doesn't need to *feel* like it! That's it!"

Before she had even fully entered the store, she spun around, hopped off the sidewalk, bounded across the street, and slipped into McHenry Hardware.

Bewildered, Nita glanced at Chrissy.

"It's a bit of a long story."

"Or a bit of a long *history*?" Nita asked rhetorically.

That was the one notable disadvantage to living in a small town—one's business was never truly their own. It was a life lived under a microscope. Or, in the case of Chrissy and Nick, a snow globe. That's how it felt to

Chrissy. She and Nick had shared this magical romance as young sweethearts, but one day it all turned upside down, everything shaken and tossed tumultuously about. She still felt that swirling disorientation, the not knowing which way was up or which way was down. She had expected everything to settle over time, but with Nick back in Heirloom Point, she felt in a constantly shaken up state.

"I'll be in the back if you need me, Nita." Chrissy gave her newest employee a brief, encouraging hug as the door opened again and a young family filtered into the shop, one by one like a row of little ducklings. "And remember to mention our buy one, get one half-off sale on the mini jars. It lasts through Wednesday."

It was a sight Chrissy never grew tired of—watching her customers lift the lids of her candles and breathe in her creations. The sense of smell was an amazing gift, the ability to transport to any time or space with just one breath. She loved helping her patrons select the perfect candle for their homes, but she would have to leave Nita to that today. She was overdue with her Christmas candle and that deadline felt like the heaviest weight on her shoulders.

As usual, the hours sped by while in the backroom, and when Nita and Everleigh announced they were clocking out for the day just before six, Chrissy had to do a double take. The only real indicator that the time was correct was the very audible grumble of her stomach, which protested loudly, not pleased with the fact that she'd worked all the way through lunch and nearly up to dinnertime. In truth, she hadn't really noticed her hunger, her constant shivering doing its best to mask it.

Everleigh had returned earlier without a heater. McHenry Hardware had a shipment coming in later in the day, but none in stock at that moment. Not that she wanted to use her inventory for kindling, but Chrissy was thankful for her candles. Even if they didn't put out much heat, there was an aura of warmth that spread from every lit wick.

Huddled in her backroom, Chrissy almost didn't hear the faint chime of the shop's door.

"Sorry, we're closed," she called out, waiting for the bells to jingle again upon exit. When that sound didn't toll, her pulsed accelerated. The patron was still there.

Heirloom Point was a safe town, but she'd heard some rattling stories from her father that she didn't wish to place herself into. It was dark and the shop was eerily quiet. Glancing around, she sought out the first thing she could locate: an old broom propped up against the far wall.

"We're closed!" she hollered again. Her fingers tightened on the handle as she rolled her shoulders and then straightened her spine, standing tall and determined. Back in high school she had taken a self defense course, but she couldn't bring to memory anything she had learned now.

Every shadow suddenly became a possible intruder, every object a threat. She knew this space intimately well, but fear and darkness unsettled her. The only available light came from the old Edison bulb that dangled in the front window and it didn't offer much in the way of illumination. The light switch for the rest of the store lighting was located on the opposite wall, far out of reach. Chrissy's throat tightened and her breath came out in shallow inhales and exhales, like she was just moments from hyperventilating.

"Hello?" Voice quivering, she caught sight of a silhouetted figure near the front of the shop. "We're closed," she said again as the intruder came fully into view. His back was rounded, his body crouched down near the floor, but he didn't even flinch at the sound of her voice. In one well-placed swing, Chrissy could knock him fully to his knees, sending him sprawling onto the ground. All she had to do was lift the broom and strike against his back. In the commotion that would ensue, she'd have time to rush out of the store to fetch help.

Raising the broom above her shoulders, she ran through the scenario in her head. When she was a young girl, she'd played a season of softball. She struck out more times than not, but she did have a powerful swing. Squaring up, she imagined she was in the batter's box again. She choked up on the broom handle and closed her eyes. Three, two...one.

The jingling door sucked all air out of her lungs. Chrissy's eyes flashed open, only to see Nick standing in the open frame, his mouth gaping, eyes wild with uncertainty. He held a large cardboard box in his hands.

"Chrissy?"

The broom released from her grasp and clattered to the floor. "Nick? What are you doing here?"

"What are *you* doing, Chrissy?"

Just then, the unknown man popped up. He yanked an earbud from his ear and wiped his hands on the front of his jeans like a mechanic would after tinkering with an engine.

"Ted?" Chrissy's chin yanked back into her scarf.

"Just thought I'd take a look at that busted radiator. Sorry—didn't think anyone was here. Your sister said she'd leave the place open for me. I didn't bother with the lights since you've got that really old one, you know? Don't want to be the guy to mess it up after all of these years. Figured I'd make do in the dark. Didn't mean to startle you."

"Oh, you didn't startle me." Chrissy attempted to regain her composure as she bent down to collect the broom. Her pulse began to decelerate to its original tempo. "I was just about to do some sweeping before I closed up for the night."

Nick shot Chrissy a sidelong glance.

"Anyway," Ted continued, "I'll need to order another part before I can fix this, so it'll be a few more days. I apologize for the inconvenience. I know it's dang cold in here."

"That's where I come in," Nick interjected as he lifted the box in his hands higher. "Brought over a space heater. Everleigh stopped by this afternoon and all but threatened to report us to the Better Business Bureau if I didn't save one for your store."

"Sounds like her."

Ted popped his headphone back in. "I'll get out of

your hair for now. When that part comes in, I'll give you a call."

"Sounds good," Chrissy said, finally letting her shoulders drop in relief. She could feel Nick's scrutinizing stare without even glancing in his direction to confirm that his eyes were set on her. "What?" she finally said, snapping her gaze his way once Ted had left the candle shop.

"Were you just about to bludgeon poor Ted with a broom handle?"

"I told you, I was going to sweep up before I clocked out."

"What exactly were you planning to sweep with a stance like that? The ceiling?"

Chrissy pursed her lips. "There are a few cobwebs."

"Okay. Sure." Nick nodded slowly. "I'll just ignore the fact that—had I not walked in at the moment I did—you would've been the newest face of Heirloom Point's Most Wanted."

"We don't even have that."

"So you would be the first then. Can't imagine that would look too good, what with your father's profession and all."

Reaching out, Chrissy took the heater from Nick. The box was heavy, but she didn't let on that it was a struggle to keep from dropping it. "Thank you for the heater, Nick. Everleigh will be very pleased. Is there anything else?"

Nick rubbed at the back of his neck and when he gave her that familiar, tentative smirk, Chrissy almost had to look away. It made her heart skip, just like it had when they were kids. "Chrissy, I'm sorry. That must've been really frightening for you."

"Only a little." Lowering the box down, Chrissy shrugged. "I'm capable of taking care of myself. I've been doing it for a long time now."

She didn't mean for the words to sound like an accusation, but it couldn't be avoided.

"I know you have." Nick took one step forward like he was about to reach for her hand, but hesitated. "I'm sorry I just showed up like this."

"You didn't just show up, Nick. Believe it or not, there's been a lot of chatter around town for a while now. I had a heads up that you were coming back to Heirloom Point, if that's what you're wondering."

"Actually, I meant I was sorry that I just showed up at your store like this." His brows drew together.

"Right," Chrissy backpedaled. "Of course."

"Sounds like we have more to talk about, though."

"I don't know, Nick. We haven't really talked for a decade."

"I know...it's just," he started. Chrissy could see the warring emotions in his eyes, hear the vacillation in his voice. "I wasn't sure if you would want to see me after all this time."

"I wasn't sure I wanted to, either. Honestly, Nick, I'm still not sure."

"I get it. It was actually your dad who suggested I speak with you."

"My dad?"

"Yeah, I chatted with him a bit this morning when I dropped off your mom's wreath."

"What are you talking about?" Chrissy's mouth bent downward. "What wreath?"

"I was at the Beasley's earlier, helping them look for a Christmas tree in their attic. We didn't find it, but I did find a wreath that had a tag with your mom's name on it. I planned to just leave it on your dad's door, but he invited me in. It was really nice, Chrissy. Being back at your old house, I don't know, it just sort of felt like old times, I guess."

"That's great that you were able to catch up with Dad, but I don't know that we can do that, Nick. Last night at the auction—talking to you felt so easy." She shrugged and her shoulders stayed scrunched up by her ears before they dropped as she sighed. "And that's the problem. I don't know how to be around you and not be *with* you, Nick. We've only ever been a couple."

"I get that, Chrissy. Believe it or not, it's been hard for me not to pull you into my arms each time I see you like I used to. I couldn't help myself last night."

That was more than Chrissy's heart could handle. "Thank you for the heater. I really do appreciate it."

She could see the glint of hope fade from Nick's eyes, slipping away ever-so-slowly until it completely vanished like the sun sinking into the horizon. "Of course." He shoved his hands deep in his pockets and added, "I suppose I'll see you around then?"

"Yep. It's a small town."

"Don't I know it."

Chrissy watched as Nick turned back toward the door. A gnawing feeling pulled at her, like a child yanking on her mother's shirtsleeve. She tried to ignore it, but the persistent tug wouldn't go away.

"Wait."

Nick spun around.

"Why did you come back to Heirloom Point, Nick?" Chrissy asked. "I mean, you could've made a life for yourself anywhere. Why here?"

"I've been everywhere, Chrissy. Sometimes the only place left to go is home." With his hand on the door handle, he offered a shrug and headed out into the cold December evening, the winter air swallowing up his words, joining the very snowflakes that fell around him.

❄

CHRISSY MADE QUICK work of closing up the shop. Nick's statement had rattled her. She knew Heirloom Point was his hometown, but she was his history, and she couldn't help but wonder if the memories of their young love were what brought him back after all of those absent years.

Sure, they had been kids when they first fell in love and over the years, Chrissy had even tried to dismiss what they had together, discounting it merely as a teenage romance. But that wasn't the truth. Nick and Chrissy had a connection unlike anything she'd ever experienced. She wasn't sure she believed in soul mates, but she did know that she had loved him from the very depths of her soul.

Still, it wasn't like they could just pick things back up, no matter how badly her heart kept trying to do so without her permission. Her head knew better. They were different people now.

Slipping her arms into her plum-colored wool coat and coiling her scarf around her neck, Chrissy gave one more sweeping glance over the candle shop before opening the door to head out for the night. The recent events had made her weary and she couldn't wait for the comforts of home. She had the key in the lock, about to button things up, when she noticed something tucked into her newly displayed wreath. It hung right at eye level. Reaching up, she pulled out a neatly folded slip of paper and read:

Fir and Spruce,
Cedar and Pine.
Holid-Hayes Tree Farm
is a forever favorite of mine.

NICK

❄

"YOU ARE A real sweetheart, Nick, coming to our rescue once again. What on earth did we do all those years without you?"

Doris patted Nick's knee in a motherly way. She was wedged right up against him in the cab of the truck, Earl sitting on the opposite side of his wife with an open newspaper in his hands, scanning the Sunday comics.

"Last night I looked over at Earl during dinner and said, 'Earl, we need a tree.'"

"To which I replied, 'Dory, my dear, then we'll need a truck.' You're really saving me here today, Nick. Tree shopping is much less stressful than truck shopping."

"You haven't been to the Hayes lot in a while, Earl," Doris quipped. "The ad on the radio said they have a dozen species to choose from! Truck shopping would most definitely be easier!" Doris turned to Nick, lowering her head to peer over her cat-eye glasses. "You picking out a tree today, too?"

"I thought I just might."

"Glad to see you're settling in, Nick. I can imagine after all that time on the road, it'll be nice to have a true, hometown Christmas. Your own tree and everything!"

"I suppose I'll have to buy some ornaments to really make it legit."

The light turned green and he lowered his foot to the pedal. He could already see a crowd forming at the tree lot two blocks ahead, everyone eager to choose from the latest evergreen shipment from Oregon.

"I always find the homemade ornaments to be my favorites. You know, I have the best recipe for the salt dough kind. Remind me to give it to you once this whole tree shopping event is behind us. You'll love it."

"You mean the ornaments that look almost edible?"

Nick remembered making that particular type with Chrissy, Everleigh, and their mother, Audrey. He had thought they were actual cookies when he walked into the kitchen one December afternoon and saw them spread out on the counter, all different holiday shapes and sizes. The girls shouted at him when he drew one to his mouth, about to snap the head off of a Santa Claus. That sweet memory made him chuckle under his breath.

"Yep, those are the ones," Doris confirmed as she pointed out the windshield. "There's a spot right over there. Put your blinker on so no one else takes it."

Nick didn't mind the copiloting. Doris was a woman with strong opinions who often made them known, but she was harmless and had good intentions. "I'm on it."

After angling his truck up against the curb and killing

the engine, Nick unbuckled the seatbelt from his lap and stepped down from the cab. He held out a hand to help Doris while Earl tucked the newspaper under his arm and exited the vehicle on the other side.

"Remember, Dory, we can't get anything taller than six feet or it will hit the ceiling once we put it in the stand. I don't want to cut the top off because you chose one that's too big for the space." Earl elbowed Nick. "I've learned to manage her expectations from the get-go," he said with a wink.

"Probably not a bad idea."

"Hurry up, you two," Doris called over her shoulder as she scooted down the walkway, negotiating the congestion of people already forming on the sidewalk. "You are both slowpokes!"

"Moving as fast as I can, dear," Earl retorted. "Not as spry as I used to be."

"Neither am I," Nick admitted. His aching knee sure kept him humble. "Let her go on ahead and we'll catch up when we can."

The lot at the end of Spruce Street was packed. It was like all of Heirloom Point had waited until this day to go on the hunt for the perfect tree. Back when Nick was a kid, he would help out at the lot during the holiday season, carrying trees for customers and tying them to vehicles, strapping them down so no branches snapped off as they whipped in the wind. It was honest, hard work but come Christmas Day, he'd often grown weary of the smell of pine and the scratched arms he'd acquired from bristly trunks and branches. But it was always fun to watch families select their holiday tree. Just like snowflakes, no two Christmas trees were alike. For some, that was overwhelming. For others, it created the perfect opportunity to find just the right match.

Consistent with Nick's memories, Tucker's younger sister, Marcie, wore a green and red elf costume and greeted each guest at the entrance with a candy cane and a welcoming smile. She was older now—a grown woman, really—but Nick figured that costume was the same one from back in the day. Its details were worn and colors faded like a church pageant costume pulled from storage and reused year after year.

"Nick McHenry!" Marcie's eyes lit up when they connected with Nick's. She raced to him to throw her arms around his neck and pull him into a hug. "It's actually you!"

"Hey, Marcie." Nick drew out of their embrace and smiled at his old friend. He'd often thought of Marcie as a younger sister and teased her like she was, too. "I see you haven't left the North Pole after all of these years."

She waved a hand up and down her outfit, adding a little twirl at the end as the finishing touch. "I really need to push my parents harder when it comes to workers' rights. I'm certain a uniform update is long overdue."

"How are your parents, anyway?"

"Same as always. We're the only lot in town, but Dad's constantly trying to improve inventory. We added the Nordmann Fir this year, even though we already have the Douglas Fir, Noble Fir, and Fraser Fir. Honestly, I think we're all going a little fir crazy around here!"

"Sounds like you've got a great selection."

"Come on down to Holid-Hayes Tree Lot for the best selection within a fifty-mile radius of Heirloom Point," Marcie rehearsed in a nasally, elfish voice.

"So that's you I heard on the radio ad?"

"You better believe it. Marcie the Elf is a bit of a local superstar. They even named the peppermint sundae down at Joyce's Diner after me. *Marcie's Merry-Mint Sundae.* Get it? Merriment?"

"Sounds like you're really moving up in the world."

She slapped a hand against Nick's shoulder. "Enough about me. You here to help out for the season, Nick?" Marcie asked, knowing full well that the Holid-Hayes Tree Lot was not the beacon which called Nick home. "It's only a small demotion in pay."

"You know, if it weren't for this knee of mine, I might actually join you all again. I have tons of great memories working this lot with you and Tuck."

"I highly doubt Mom and Dad could compete with your current paycheck."

"Oh, you just might be surprised."

Marcie paused briefly to grin at customers who passed through the entrance and then angled her attention back to Nick. "Chrissy's over near the Douglas Firs if you're looking for her."

"Chrissy's here?" Nick couldn't mask the surprise in his tone.

"Oh." Eyes wide, Marcie looked as though she had spoken out of turn. "I'm sorry. I figured you were meeting her here."

"No. I'm actually here with the Beasleys. They needed a truck to get their tree home, so I volunteered mine."

"I'm sorry, Nick. I just assumed..." Marcie's voice trailed off.

"It's okay, Marcie. No harm, no foul." Stepping forward to allow a couple through the tight entrance, Nick nearly knocked into a giant plastic candy cane. "I'll let you get back to your elf responsibilities. Catch up later?"

"Sure thing. Sounds great!"

The lot was an evergreen labyrinth. Trees of every conceivable variation dotted the asphalt. There were ones as wide as they were tall and others that hardly tapered, resembling cylinders more than triangular peaks.

He didn't feel like he was intentionally on the lookout for her, but when Nick suddenly wandered his way toward the selection of flocked trees, he knew his subconscious had guided him there. One row over, admiring a looming, fake-snow covered fir, was Chrissy, a look of adoration on her face.

"It's a nice tree," Nick spoke, interjecting into her reverie.

Chrissy's head whipped up. "Oh, Nick! You startled me!" She collected her composure as she breathed out through her mouth. "I wasn't sure what time you would be here."

Nick hadn't remembered mentioning his plans to take Doris and Earl tree shopping, but he must have said something the previous night in passing. How else would Chrissy know he would be there?

"Do you like this one?" Chrissy's gaze switched back to the tree between them. "I know you never liked flocked trees, but there's just something so cozy about them. This particular one is lovely, isn't it?"

"It's not that I don't like them—"

"Nick McHenry. I vividly remember you saying they look like they're coated in shreds of toilet paper. If that doesn't suggest that you are not a fan, then I don't know what does."

"I'll admit they're not my favorite, but more for the mess they create than anything." The last thing Nick wanted to do was hurt Chrissy's feelings over Christmas tree preferences. Things already felt strained enough.

"We're allowed to have different likes and dislikes, Nick. In fact, we've always been a bit opposite."

"I think that's why we worked so well. Opposites attract and all." Nick noticed the faint smile slip from Chrissy's mouth, and when her gaze fell downward as she busied her hands with a lose string on her mittens, he knew he had said too much. It was clear he'd made her uncomfortable. "I think this tree is perfect for you, Chrissy."

Her eyes lifted up and relief highlighted her features. "I think so, too. I can picture it decorated and on display already. Those big bay windows are going to frame it in perfectly."

"Bay windows?"

"At the house." She looked suddenly anxious, like

she'd overshared. "You don't know? I bought the Miller home a few years back."

"Oh. Wow." Nick swallowed. That information certainly hadn't traveled to Newcastle. "That's really great, Chrissy."

She lifted a mitten-clad hand and fiddled with a branch on the tree between them. "I figured you had heard."

"I hadn't, but I'm serious, that's really great. I'm happy for you."

"Thank you." She smiled at him, but it didn't reach her eyes. "It's much more of a fixer upper than we ever suspected."

"Oh yeah?"

"Remember how we said the first thing we would do was hang a swing on that old porch?" Nick nodded, the many conversations still tangible in his memory. Chrissy continued, "Well, I did just that, but it turned out the entire porch needed redoing. For some time, that swing was suspended a good twelve feet off the ground with nothing underneath it. Like those rides at the fair. You know the kind I'm talking about? With the swings that twirl out when it spins?"

"I can totally picture that." Nick forced a half smile. "I bet that was a monumental task, redoing an entire deck."

"Thankfully, I had a lot of help. Kevin was a godsend. Apparently, he retained more information from our high school woodshop class than I ever did."

Nick froze at the mention of his brother's name. "Kevin helped you?"

"He did. Honestly, I don't know what I would've done without him. He sort of became the unofficial foreman for our ragtag crew of construction volunteers. I'm still so surprised he chose to spend all of his leave restoring that old house."

Nick shoved his hands into his coat pockets. This was new information and he couldn't put the pieces in any sort of order that made sense. "Kevin never mentioned it."

"Maybe he didn't want to…" Chrissy's voice faded, appearing to struggle to find the words.

"Didn't want to tell me he was restoring my dream home? With you?"

Pulling her chin back, Chrissy bristled. "It wasn't like that, Nick."

Nick shut his eyes for a moment and drew in a breath of air that hurt his lungs. He manufactured a smile and forced his mind to stop wandering into territory it had no business wandering. "I'd love to come by and see it sometime, Chrissy. I'm sure you've turned it into something beautiful."

Eyebrows raised, a relieved grin lifted the corners of Chrissy's mouth. "I'd be happy to give you the tour. There are still some things that will eventually need updating, but I'm pleased with how it turned out. I think you would like it, too."

"I'm sure I would."

Their gaze held for a beat longer than what felt

comfortable and the dry tickle forming in Nick's throat required a cough to clear. He broke from their locked stare. "I should probably go check on Doris and Earl. I have a sneaking suspicion their trip to the tree lot might require a referee."

"That sounds about right." She laughed. "Go on and catch up with them. And be sure to tell them I said hi."

"Will do." Nick turned on his heel to go, but before leaving Chrissy he said, "I think this tree is perfect for you and I agree, it will be beautiful framed by those windows. You really can't go wrong."

CHRISSY

CHRISSY HAD A plan. She would be the one to pack up and leave this time. Not permanently, of course, because she had a shop to run and candles to make. But Everleigh could handle things during the busy holiday season just fine. And as it turned out, she had hired Nita at the perfect time. They would hardly even notice Chrissy's absence.

She dialed her sister's number and clicked on the speaker button, then settled the phone onto the center console of her sedan. After three rings, Everleigh picked up.

"Yell-o," Everleigh greeted cheerily.

"Ev, I've got a favor to ask."

"Sure thing. You name it."

Tapping her thumbs on the steering wheel as she waited for the traffic light to turn green, Chrissy blurted, "I'm leaving Heirloom Point for the unforeseeable future.

I'll need you to man things at the candle shop until I get back."

A pause so long she could hear the static on the line followed. Then, in the most serious voice, Everleigh answered, "I'll be right over with my shovel."

"Shovel?" Chrissy lowered her foot to the gas pedal and cruised through the intersection, heading toward her home with her newly purchased, flocked Christmas tree strapped to the roof. "Why do you need a shovel?"

"Because there's obviously something that you need help covering up. That's the only plausible explanation as to why you would leave town in such a hurry, Chrissy. You've committed some terrible crime and gotta get the heck outta Dodge. And since I'm such a fabulous sister, I'll help you out—*and* I won't even tell Dad I did all the dirty work."

"Stop being crazy, Ev."

"I'm not the crazy one, sis," Everleigh reasoned. "You and I both know neither of us will ever leave Heirloom Point. We're lifers."

"I'm not so sure about that anymore."

Everleigh sighed through the phone. "This whole Nick homecoming is really throwing you off, isn't it?"

"It's done more than throw me off. It's knocked me completely down. Life was so simple. So predictable. And now it's neither of those two things."

"Simple and predictable don't sound like the most exciting adjectives when it comes to describing one's life. It might not be all bad that things have been shaken up a bit. Keeps life exciting, if you ask me."

"There was nothing exciting in seeing Nick's expression when he found out I bought the Miller place," Chrissy offered as she flipped on her turn signal to angle her vehicle down Cresleigh Street at the edge of town. Looming proud and tall at the end of the road was the one-hundred-twenty-year-old Victorian home she had used every penny of her savings to purchase. She still got a warm, fuzzy feeling each time the majestic structure came into view.

"I always wondered if word ever got back to him about that," Everleigh said.

"Nope. It didn't. And it never got back to him that Kevin was the one to help with the restoration, either."

"Ouch." Chrissy could hear Everleigh pop something into her mouth and crunch down loudly. Apparently Chrissy had caught her during lunch. "You have to try to see things from his perspective, Chris. It has to be a huge adjustment to come back to Heirloom Point after all those years on the road. Don't you think the knowledge that you bought that house makes Nick feel like you just kept on living out the life he'd left behind?"

"That's not how it is," Chrissy said indignantly.

"I know it's not, but that might be how it comes across. You need to put yourself in his hockey skates and try to see things from Nick's point of view."

"This isn't the pep-talk I was hoping for." Killing the engine after she pulled up to the house, Chrissy sat deeply in her seat and ran a frustrated hand through her hair. She took the phone off of speaker and held it to her ear. "I was just calling to ask for a small, teeny, tiny favor."

"Right. Sorry, sis, but I'm not about to let you make some irrational, life-altering decision just because you're uncomfortable that your ex is in town."

When put that way, Chrissy could see the absurdity in it all. Why had their reunion made her act this way? It wasn't like her. "What I don't understand is why he'd ask me to meet him at the tree lot and then act so surprised to see me there. It just doesn't make any sense."

"Nick asked you to go to the lot with him?"

"Well, not in those exact words. But he left a note in the candle shop wreath last night after he dropped off the heater. It all but invited me to go."

"He dropped off a heater?" Everleigh screamed so loudly Chrissy had to pull the phone away to keep from bursting an eardrum. "That man is an angel!"

"Ev, focus."

"I'm sorry, sis, but you have no idea how excited I am that I won't lose my fingers to frostbite during my shift tomorrow," her sister explained. "Anyway. There was a note to meet at the tree lot? That's really sweet. Maybe it's his way of easing back into a friendship with you, Chrissy. I think you shouldn't read into it so much and just roll with it. He's obviously trying to make amends in the best way he knows how."

Maybe Everleigh was right. Maybe Chrissy was reading into things too much. Maybe Nick wasn't even that surprised to learn about her house and all the time she'd spent with his brother during his absence.

But she knew that look that fell across his features, the one that displayed his sheer shock to find out that she'd purchased the Miller home—the home they'd mapped out an entire future to take place within. Of course she often wondered what it would be like to share this space with Nick. As young loves, they would take the long way home just to steal a glimpse of the historic home. Other than Prosper Tomlin's farm, it was one of the few spaces in Heirloom Point that still had any acreage. Like most communities, large properties had been parceled off over the years, with smaller homes erected where grand structures once stood.

Nick had promised Chrissy that the Miller home would one day be theirs. He would play a few years of hockey at whatever level he could just to save enough money to secure their dream. When the home finally came on the market a few years back, Chrissy had thought seriously about calling Nick to share the news of its availability.

But if their love hadn't been enough to pull Nick back to Heirloom Point, an empty house certainly wouldn't do any better a job.

"Listen," Everleigh spoke into the reflective silence that grew in their phone conversation. "What are you doing right now? Sounds like you could use a pick me up."

"I was just planning to schlep this tree into the house and get it set up. Not much going on other than that."

"Save the schlepping until I'm there. Tree schlepping

is definitely a two-woman job. I'll even bring hot chocolate. See what a good sister I am?"

Chrissy couldn't disagree. Everleigh was the best. "I love you, Ev."

"I know you do."

❄

"IT SMELLS LIKE it's burning." Chrissy scrunched her nose and grimaced.

"Popcorn always smells like it's burning when it's popping. It's totally fine."

The trill of the smoke detector confirmed Chrissy's suspicions. "Pretty sure it's burning!" Racing into the kitchen, Chrissy threw open the microwave door and grabbed a nearby towel that had been folded up next to the dish rack. She flapped the cloth against the streams of thick smoke which billowed, making the surrounding space an opaque cloud of gray.

Everleigh let out a choked cough. "Okay. You may be right. I think it is burning."

"That was my last bag of popcorn." Chrissy held the charred bag by the corner and slumped against the island. "Now what are we going to use for garland?"

"We were using it for garland? I thought we were making ourselves a little afternoon snack." Everleigh looked disappointed. "I don't think you're supposed to put popcorn garland on a flocked tree anyway, sis. That feels like all kinds of fake snow overkill."

Chrissy shrugged. "It's the way I always do it."

"Well, maybe it's time to do things a bit differently." She took her sister by the arms and offered an encouraging grin. "What else do you have that we could use? Something you have a lot of that would look decent when wrapped around a tree."

Chrissy couldn't think. She had been in a tizzy since her run-in with Nick that morning and even though she thought setting up and decorating her tree would provide the calm she needed, she found herself more stressed than anything. From the box of glass ornaments she'd dropped and broken during her climb down from the attic to the recent popcorn fiasco, nothing seemed to be going Chrissy's way.

"I don't know. I've got a lot of candles."

"Yeah, um, no. We've already had one thing go up in smoke today. We don't need to incinerate an entire tree. What else?"

"Macaroni?"

"If you were a preschool teacher, sure, that could work, but that's not the case here. Any other options?"

"I have tons of cranberries left over from Thanksgiving. I never got around to making the sauce and opted to buy the canned kind instead."

"Yes!" Everleigh's eyes lit up. "That's perfect. Those things last for weeks. Got some needles?"

"I do. In the back room with my sewing kit."

"And fishing line?"

The excitement dropped from Chrissy's face. "That, I don't have."

"It's fine. We'll just make a quick pit stop to McHenry's," Everleigh said. "Go grab your jacket. I'll drive."

Chrissy didn't attempt to protest, knowing her sister wouldn't let her out of it easily. Nick probably wouldn't even be there. On Sundays, McHenry Hardware closed up early and since he was at the tree lot just a few hours earlier, she doubted he would go in for an afternoon shift. Plus, she didn't know if he even officially worked for his parents now that he was back. She didn't know much of Nick's plans, really.

Everleigh grabbed her purse and keys from the kitchen table and headed toward the front door. "Ready?" Like she could read her sister's hesitation, she said, "Come on—I'll be your buffer if Nick's there."

"Somehow that doesn't instill huge amounts of confidence."

"Oh come on, sis. I'm the master of distractions. Do you have any idea how many people I was able to redirect when they came over to look at my candy cane wreath? Everyone wanted a piece of it." Then squinting and pursing her lips, Everleigh added, "Matter of fact, remind me to pick up another wreath while we're at the store. My door looks empty without one."

"You ate that entire wreath already?" Chrissy asked as she bounded down the porch steps behind your sister.

"I told you it would be gone in a matter of days." Everleigh turned back and winked. "You should know by now I'm a woman of my word."

NICK

THE SNOW HAD just started to fall, despite the weatherman's predictions for clear skies.

Through the hardware store windows, Nick could see the cottony layer clinging to the ledges and roofline of Chrissy's candle shop across the way. At least her store was closed on Sundays. One awkward encounter per day was plenty sufficient.

"Didn't expect snow today." Nick's dad, Joe, narrowed his gaze and squinted through his glasses as he took in Spruce Street. "Think there'll be enough for Slushy to make his first appearance of the season?"

Nick grinned. For years, he and his father built a snowman on the sidewalk just outside the hardware store when a decent winter storm made it possible. Instead of coal and carrots, they used items found within the shop. Bolts and washers for the eyes. A funnel nose. PVC pipes for the arms and a weed paper scarf. It was a silly tradition that started when Nick was just a small boy, but it was one he held dear.

"I think we'll need a few more big storms before we have enough snow to work with, but I, for one, can't wait for Slushy's arrival."

"Always could count on you to play along." Joe clamped a hand down on his youngest son's shoulder. "Kevin never did take any interest in making that silly snowman."

Nick muted the thought that was about to form, the one that wondered if maybe Kevin had been too busy taking an interest in other things. His brother was a good, honorable man. He didn't deserve Nick's scrutiny.

"It'll sure be nice to have both of my boys here for Christmas this year. I can't even remember the last time all four of us shared a holiday meal together. Must be ten years or more."

"Kevin's coming home for Christmas?"

"Yep. Your mother just got the phone call this morning. Haven't seen her so happy in years. I think I might even get out of buying her a gift this year because nothing's going to top having both of her boys under one roof for the holidays."

The bell chiming above the door pulled Nick out of the conversation. He was relieved to see Everleigh walk through the entrance, but that relief didn't last more than a few seconds. Chrissy trailed behind, her cheeks reddened from the icy air and her dark hair dusted with fine, powdery snowflakes. She looked alarmingly beautiful. Shivering, she shook out her hands and ran them up and down her arms. When their eyes locked across the store, Nick felt that same shiver creep down his spine.

"Davenport ladies, what can I help you with this wintery afternoon? Did that heater make its way over to you last night?" Joe asked, stepping toward the women.

"Sure did," Everleigh said. "Thank you for that. It'll be so nice not to freeze during my shift at the shop. We're actually here for some fishing line. Would you be able to point us in the right direction?"

"Absolutely," Joe said with a nod. "Right this way."

Everleigh followed, but Chrissy hesitated, her gaze still fastened on Nick. Slowly, she paced toward the cash register where he stood as he counted the day's sales from the drawer. She fiddled with the fringe of her wool scarf and then flashed a brief, guarded smile as her only greeting.

"You plan on doing a little ice fishing?" Nick joked, but it felt forced and unnatural. He thumbed through the stack of dollar bills in his hand and counted them out under his breath.

"The one and only time I've ever fished was during that church retreat back when we were juniors. Remember? Camp Awanagohem?"

"Oh yeah." Nick bundled the dollars with a rubber band and moved on to the fives. "Camp *I Wanna Go Home* was a better name for it, though."

"You're just sore because I won first place in the trout competition and yours came in dead last."

"Of course I was sore over it. As you just admitted, it

was the one and only time you'd ever fished. It was probably the hundredth time I had."

"You've always had such a competitive nature, Nick."

"I know. Sometimes I think I need to learn how to reel it in," he joked, pleased with the unexpected pun.

"I see what you did there," Chrissy acknowledged with a chuckle. "I think your competitive nature has served you quite well. I mean, it takes more than just talent to make it to the pros. You've got grit and determination and those are admirable qualities."

Shutting the register drawer, Nick shook his head. "Until they're not." He dropped his hands onto the counter. "Listen, Chrissy. I want to apologize for how I behaved back at the tree lot. I think a little of that competitive nature came out when you told me Kevin helped with the house and that just wasn't right. I'm sorry."

Chrissy shook her head quickly. "It wasn't like that at all, Nick."

"I know it wasn't. Which is why I want to apologize. And even if it was, it's not something I should have an opinion about, anyway."

"Kevin has always been there for me—"

"I know." The smile fell from his mouth. "And I wasn't."

"I was going to say Kevin has always been there for me like a big brother. That's it," Chrissy corrected.

"Still, it just never occurred to me that Kevin would be the one repairing that old porch or stripping the wallpaper from the dining room or retiling the bathroom floor. Those were things I figured I would do, I suppose."

"It's a little hard to renovate a house from two-thousand miles away," Chrissy said around a quick laugh. "But you were where you were supposed to be, Nick."

"And now? Do you think this is where I'm supposed to be?"

"I think only you can answer that."

"Got the fishing line!" Everleigh's booming voice forced a quick end to their conversation. She bounded up to the counter. "How much do I owe you?"

"It's on the house," Joe said as he rounded the checkout stand and grabbed a brown bag for Everleigh to place the item into. "We're closing up soon anyway and I'm sure Nick doesn't want to rebalance the register."

"Well, thank you, Joe," Everleigh said. "I appreciate it."

The sisters turned to go, but Chrissy stopped right before the store's threshold and spun around. "Can I add my two cents?"

"Not if it's going to throw off the register," Nick joked, knowing it was a particularly bad one.

Smiling sweetly, Chrissy paused, then said, "I think it might throw off more than that, so I'll just keep it to myself for now."

※

"DID YOU KNOW Kevin helped restore the old Miller place?"

Nick handed Tucker a bottle of root beer over the back of the sofa and cracked one open for himself. He placed the opener onto the counter and grabbed a bag of potato chips from the cupboard to satisfy his salt craving. The Northern Lights game was just about to start, but Nick's television was still on mute.

"Yeah, I did, but only because I helped with it, too." Tucker took a long swig from the amber bottle. "That place was a dump, Moose. You should be glad your dream of owning it never came to fruition. I can't even imagine the amount of money poor Chrissy dumped into it."

"Did a lot of people help out?" The more he settled into Heirloom Point, the more unsettled Nick grew. It was easy to pretend things had stayed the same in his absence, but houses and lives were rebuilt and he hadn't been any part of it.

"Yeah, there were a few of us. Me, Kevin, Lee, your dad. I think Earl even came by a few times, but Doris always seemed to have a reason to pull him away." Tucker reached across the couch to retrieve the remote. He cranked up the volume. The roar of the stands filled the room and Nick's heart lurched into a faster pace. Like déjà vu, he was instantly back in that hockey rink. The sights. The smells. The sounds. It was all right there, vivid and real as though he could feel the very ice underneath his feet. "Hey." Tucker narrowed his eyes at his friend. "You okay, buddy?"

"I'm good." Nick took a swig of soda and plopped down onto the couch. "You won't think I'm crazy if I admit that I haven't watched a game since my contract ended, will you?"

Tucker angled the remote at the screen. "I'll shut it off. We don't need to watch this. I can catch up on the stats tomorrow."

"No, no. It's fine. It just feels like another life, you know?" Nick sat forward to place his drink onto the coffee table. He grabbed a handful of chips from the open bag and then leaned back. "But *this* feels like another life, too, so I don't really know what that leaves me with."

"Looks like you get the chance to create a totally new life. I don't know, buddy. To me, that sounds pretty exciting."

"If I'm being completely real, coming home makes me wish I'd never left," Nick admitted. He tossed the chips into his mouth. "Like if I had known *this*"—he glanced down at his injured knee—"would be the outcome of pursuing hockey, I think I would've stayed here and never left at all."

"Nah, man. Then you never would've realized your dream."

"As it stands, I think I actually missed out on a much greater one."

Remote still in his grip, Tucker clicked the sound off. The room fell silent. He rotated on the couch to face his friend. "I see what you're getting at, and Nick, I'm going to tell it to you straight: just ask her out."

"I can't do that, Tuck."

"Why not? Because it's been a decade since your last date?"

"Because it's been a decade since we called off our engagement. That's a little different. I can't just waltz back into town and act like that never happened."

"Yeah, you're right. I've seen you dance. I don't recommend waltzing anywhere. But in all seriousness, I think she'd say yes to a simple date, Nick. It's pretty harmless."

"Why would she say yes to a date?" Nick reached for his drink.

"Because deep down, I think she still has feelings for you. I think it's the real reason why things never went anywhere with Kevin."

Nick nearly choked on his root beer. "What never went anywhere with Kevin?"

"Any sort of relationship. Plus, I think he got tired of being rejected. That poor guy must've asked her out at least a half-dozen times when we were working on the house." Tucker switched his attention to the flat-screen TV hanging on the wall and turned the sound back on at a low volume. "A half-dozen that I'm aware of. Probably more."

"Kevin asked Chrissy out?"

"Yeah."

Tucker's eyes were glued to the game which was now underway. Nick's old teammates flashed across the screen, their blue and red jerseys a blur of color as their skates carved deep grooves into the ice. Hockey sticks slammed together and bodies crashed against one another, along with the rink walls.

"This is all news to me."

"What? That your brother asked your ex-fiancé out? Repeatedly?" Tucker's mouth flattened into a line. "Okay, now that I say it out loud, it does sound pretty crazy. Listen man, it really was nothing. It's not like he stood any chance with her. Chrissy hasn't been in any real relationship since you left."

Relief should have followed that statement. Nick didn't anticipate the guilt that ensued instead. He had wanted Chrissy to move on and to find love again. He'd wanted it for himself, too, but it never happened. No woman could ever compare.

Nick half-watched the game, but each scored goal only made him focus on a different goal: to make things right with Chrissy.

For that, he would need to come up with an entirely new game plan.

CHRISSY

T HE TREE WASN'T an eyesore, but it certainly wouldn't be gracing the cover of any holiday home magazine. Chrissy wished she hadn't dropped that box of ornaments, and not just because it left her with a sparsely decorated tree. Those particular ornaments had been her mother's, some of the few things she had left of hers. It wasn't like they were handed down in some heartfelt ceremony. In fact, her mom had wanted to donate them, but offered them to Chrissy at the last moment.

Chrissy wasn't particularly fond of them—they were just silver and gold glass balls, nothing special—but at the time, she grasped onto anything her mother passed her way. Audrey had been sick for a couple of years at that point and Chrissy found herself clinging to any and everything having to do with her mother, whether that be a box of old, secondhand ornaments, or her sage advice.

What she wouldn't give to be able to call her mom and ask her opinion on things with Nick. Audrey had always loved Nick, but she also knew the heartbreak Chrissy experienced when he left to pursue his hockey career. As moms often do, Audrey had picked up her daughter's pieces and kept her moving forward, encouraging new hobbies and interests. It was around then that the two decided to open up the candle shop. Audrey had a high school friend back east who had just launched her own small business and a visit out to her store was all the encouragement Audrey needed to set her mind on something similar for Heirloom Point.

Chrissy had always loved candles, so she required little convincing. A candle could represent so many things. They were romantic when placed in the center of a beautifully set dining table. They were cozy when flickering on a Christmas hearth. They provided light when things seemed dark, and they twinkled during long, endless storms.

And they smelled so good. That was probably Chrissy's favorite part.

Curling her hand around her mug of cider, Chrissy drew in a slow, simmering sip. Her holiday drink reminded her of one of her candles from a few years back: *Merry Mulled Christmas Cider.* She had sold out of that candle in three days flat. Everyone seemed to love the rich, earthy aroma. She was starting to worry that she'd never come up with something new for this year, let alone top the success of that particular candle.

Hoping to relax and forget about her candle deadline for the night, Chrissy made plans to cozy up with a book and read by the fireplace and recently setup Christmas tree, but her brain couldn't focus on the words on the page. Paragraph after paragraph muddled into one another until Chrissy had turned several pages without recalling anything that had happened. She shut her book and discarded it to the side table.

She glanced around the room. How she loved this space, mostly for the massive picture windows that took in all of Cresleigh Street. When she had renovated the home, she had wanted to keep many original elements, while at the same time bringing the house's efficiency up to modern times. She adored the old Victorian for the detailed crown molding and the high ceilings. It felt rich and opulent, which was ironic considering the money pit the home turned out to be. Somehow, Chrissy made things work, but the restoration had drained her savings account. That made her uneasy. Living paycheck to paycheck wasn't her ideal plan, but sometimes life didn't go according to plan.

Looking out the windows, Chrissy admired the lights that shone brightly from her neighbors' rooflines and gutters. Some pulsed with holiday music and others glowed a steady, white brilliance. She appreciated that everyone took the time to decorate their homes for the holidays. There wasn't a single Scrooge to be found in her neighborhood.

With her mediocre tree center stage, framed in by those prominent windows, she realized she needed to put in a little more effort in the decorating department. There was no sense in showcasing something so uninspiring.

The tree needed a theme, one that involved more than just simple, strung cranberries.

Chrissy had been grateful for Everleigh's suggestion, and even more grateful for the help in making the garland. Just like her burned fingertips during the wreath making, Everleigh managed to jab her finger on multiple occasions while she pierced the cranberries with the needle. Chrissy began to wonder if her sister needed glasses; she seemed so accident prone lately.

Laughing to herself, Chrissy almost didn't hear the rap on the front door. Another louder knock had her rising to her feet.

"Hope I'm not bothering you." Chrissy's father stood on the threshold, a small crockpot in his grip and a wide grin under his mustache. "Sandra dropped off some stew at the station today and there's more than we can all eat. Have you had dinner yet?"

"I haven't." Lee lifted the lid to the pot and the hearty aroma wafted out. Chrissy's stomach growled on cue. "That smells amazing. Thanks for thinking of me, Dad. I'd love some."

Walking through the foyer toward the kitchen, Lee placed the pot onto the marble island and reached into the cupboards to retrieve two bowls.

"You're doing me a favor," Lee said with a wink as he opened the cutlery drawer and took out two soup spoons. "I think Miss Sandra is trying to fatten me up. This is the third meal she's brought by this week."

"I think that woman is interested in more than fattening you up, Dad."

"What do you mean by that?"

Lee ladled a hefty scoop into each bowl and carried them to the dining table where Chrissy joined him. She handed him an embroidered cloth napkin and then sat down.

"I think she's got a crush on you," she said.

Lee flapped the napkin at his daughter. "That's ridiculous. We're just friends. Known each other forever."

"Yes, but you're a bachelor now."

"I certainly don't feel like a bachelor."

"I know you don't. But I think enough time has gone by since Mom passed that people figure you're in the market again, you know? And maybe enough time *has* passed. Have you thought about dating at all?"

Leaning back in his chair, Lee thumbed his chin. "Sure. I suppose I've thought about it. But Chrissy, I wouldn't even know how to ask a woman out. It's been over thirty years since I've had to do that."

"I get it, Dad. I do. It's been a decade since I've been in any sort of relationship and the thought of going on a date now gives me tons of anxiety."

"You're thinking about dating again?"

Chrissy swallowed down the bite of stew in her mouth and ran her napkin across her lips. "I don't know. I think I might've misspoke. I'm not really thinking about dating again, it's just, with Nick being back and all…"

"Do you think there's still something there?" Something shifted in her father's gaze, a glint of hope alight in his eye. Lee tilted his head.

Chrissy sighed. She didn't want to get anyone's hopes up, least of all, her dad's. She knew he had once thought of Nick as a son. "I don't know, Dad. I mean, yeah, there's always been something. I loved him for a long time. I wasn't ready to end things." She couldn't trap the tear that formed. She thrust her thumb to her eye to swipe it away before it had the chance to fall.

Lee reached across the table and covered his daughter's hand with his. "Chrissy, if there's anyone who understands that, it's me."

"Gosh, Dad. I'm so sorry. I'm being really insensitive." She sniffed back any other tears that threatened to spill.

"No, you're not. You had an entire life planned with Nick and that ended. Just like mine ended with Mom."

"Things ended because we chose to end it, even if deep down, I didn't want to. It's sad that it did, but it was still a choice." Chrissy mindlessly twirled her spoon in the stew. "Things with Mom—there wasn't any choice involved there."

"I get that the circumstances were different, but a broken heart is a broken heart," Lee said, looking at his daughter with affection. "Listen, as a father, all I want in this life is to see my girls happy."

"I am happy, Dad. I love my candle shop. I love this house. This town. There's so much to love about my life."

"And maybe there's an opportunity for even *more*. That's all I'm saying. Don't wall yourself off when it comes to love, Chrissy. There's always room for more."

❄

CHRISSY COULDN'T LIE. It was nice to have a working heater in the shop again, even if it was only a space heater and even if it only warmed up about three feet of the store at a time. She cozied up next to it in the back room for most of the morning and savored each moment it oscillated her direction, warming her with a gust of hot air.

She had arrived early after a night of tossing and turning. Sleep eluded her. The delicious stew her dad brought over sat well with her, but the conversation hadn't. Even Chrissy's father seemed to be glad that Nick was in town again. Was she the only one who hadn't come to that conclusion yet?

"Mornin' Sunshine!" Everleigh burst through the door with a sing-song shout. "Actually, there isn't any sun to speak of, but Mornin' Snowstorm doesn't have the same ring to it." She caught sight of Chrissy who came out to greet her. "Hmm," Everleigh muttered, noticing her sister's scowl. "Snowstorm might be a more fitting greeting for you based on the glare you're shooting at me right now."

Chrissy's eyes zeroed in on the white sheet of paper in her sister's hands. "What is that?"

"Oh, this?" Everleigh held up the note. "I found it stuffed in your wreath. Looks like another note."

"Give it here." Chrissy flapped her hands at her sister, requesting the piece of paper.

Everleigh lifted it high, like a game of keep away.

"What? Do you have a secret admirer? Is this a *love* letter? Is that what this is?"

"Just let me see it."

Arm still stretched, Everleigh unfolded the sheet and began to read aloud:

It's a tradition that's been held for many generations,
Where we collect our coats and head down to the station.
So gather up all of your holiday donations
And don't miss out on this town-wide celebration!

"That's right!" Everleigh folded the letter and handed it to her sister. "The coat drive is today. Weird that someone would send out a reminder, but I guess it's necessary because I, for one, totally forgot. Gotta raid my closet and see what I can part with."

Chrissy's heart sank. Maybe that's exactly what these notes were: friendly reminders of Heirloom Point traditions. Why had she assumed she was the only one to receive them? It was a naïve hope to believe they were from Nick. Plus, there wasn't anything even remotely romantic or date-worthy about a clothing drive. Not that a trip to the tree lot was considered romantic, either, but Chrissy sure did have some fond memories of visiting Nick while he worked there back in the day.

"You seem disappointed," Everleigh said. "Were you hoping it was something else?"

Chrissy folded the paper. "No. No." She shook her head. "I figured it was probably some sort of notice.

Anyway, I should get back to work. This holiday candle won't create itself!"

"I'm beginning to think you won't create it either," Everleigh teased.

"You might not be wrong."

Laughing, Everleigh snickered, "I'm never wrong."

NICK

"THERE'S A BARREL by the door. Would you check to see what we've got in there so far?" Grace asked her son as she looked up from the inventory clipboard in her hands.

Working at the hardware store wasn't Nick's dream for this new chapter in his life, but the holidays were their busiest times and they needed all the extra help they could get. Nick looked at it as a transition period until he figured out how he wanted to spend his days. For now, it paid the rent and he even enjoyed the extra time spent with his mom and dad. It was a literal Mom and Pop Shop and he was grateful they'd been able to keep it running all of these years. That hadn't been the case for all stores like this, and he knew it was a blessing that its doors were still open.

Peering into the donation barrel, Nick was shocked to see it stuffed to the brim with new and slightly worn coats and jackets. He couldn't count them all just by looking, but he guessed there were upwards of twenty crammed into the bin.

Grace came up behind him. "Wow! Look at that! You're going to have your arms full!" She reached in and started to retrieve the coats from the large tub, pulling them out one by one and shoving them into her son's arms. "Take these on down to the station for me, will you?"

The Heirloom Point Police Station was just a block up from McHenry Hardware. It made no sense to load things into a car and drive, but there were more jackets than Nick could carry in one trip. And the snow had been falling steadily all afternoon, coating the pavement with a thin, but hazardous, overlay of sleet. He had visions of tumbling down the sidewalk while negotiating such a load. At least he would have plenty of cushioning to pad his fall.

Grace seemed to get a kick out of stuffing the coats into her son's arms, giggling the entire way through. When she ran out of room, she draped them over his shoulders, and even used the hood of one jacket to hang from his head. Stepping back, she covered her mouth as she took in the sight.

"That's perfect!" She couldn't contain the laugh at the end of her words.

"I look like the Pillsbury Dough Boy."

"Yes! That's exactly what you look like, but it's all for a good cause." She shooed him with her clipboard after she picked it back up, ready to continue her work. "Now get on down to the station before this storm gets worse. We're expected to get six more inches by nightfall."

Waddling his way toward the door, Nick shook his head, but doing so caused the jackets to slip, so he kept his outward grumbling to a minimum. As his mom had said, it was all for a good cause.

Keeping his gaze forward, Nick reached for the handle and opened the door, careful to maintain purpose-fully slow strides so as not to drop everything onto the slush-coated pavement. The air that rushed at him was stinging cold, but with all the layers, Nick scarcely felt it. In fact, with each step, he found himself working up a sweat. His knee bothered him again—always seemed to lately—and it didn't care that he had such a precarious task ahead of him. He ignored the ache and looked straight ahead toward the brick station at the end of the block, needing to focus on a goal. Luckily, the town square was quiet and empty, the rest of the population wise enough to stay indoors. He really didn't want any spectators for this particular task.

It took three times as long as it should have, but Nick reached the station intact, every jacket still in place. He was unreasonably proud about that. Through the glass door, Lee caught sight of Nick ambling up the walk and rushed forward to open it before he had a chance to.

"Hey there, buddy," Lee greeted. "Looks like you've got your arms full. Let me get that for you."

Tumbling into the lobby, Nick breathed a huge sigh of relief. He thought his hockey uniform had a lot of padding, but this took the cake. "I'm here with our store's donations," Nick said cheerily, even if it wasn't as heart-felt as he hoped. "Where should I put them?"

Nick turned around as the door opened again.

It was Chrissy, and when she took in the ridiculous sight, she pinned her lips between her teeth to stifle the laugh Nick knew was coming. He couldn't blame her. He looked absurd.

"Hey, Nick," she said as her mouth edged into a slow smile. "That is you in there, isn't it?"

"I think so," Nick answered. "Somewhere in here."

"Let's get those off of you, son. Must be getting awfully toasty." Lee stepped forward and took Nick's shoulders into his grasp as he navigated him toward the row of barrels lined up along the south wall. "We can put everything in those collection barrels."

"Adding casters to the barrels sure seems to have made it easier for store owners to drop off their donations, Dad," Chrissy said, that grin deepening on her face. "That was a smart idea. They just wheel them right on down the street and *presto*! All done."

Nick gulped back his embarrassment and laughed. "All the barrels have wheels on the bottom?"

"Sure do," Lee said as he removed the jackets—one by one—from Nick's silly ensemble. "It was your mom's idea, actually. Your store supplied them, too. Really nice of your parents."

"So this whole getup"—Nick waved a hand up and down his body—"was purely for my mom's entertain-ment. I could have just wheeled our barrel on over?"

"Seems to be the case," Lee said, grinning.

"And for our entertainment, too," Chrissy chimed in. "I'm glad I decided to come down here when I did. I wouldn't want to miss this."

Nick looked over at her now that he could move more easily without the cumbersome layers. "Where's your donation barrel, Chrissy?"

Like she'd seen the Ghost of Christmas Past, Chrissy's face drained of color. "My barrel?"

"Yeah, your collection for the coat drive? You didn't just wheel yours on down the street like everyone else?"

Stammering, she swallowed and then said, "I just have the one," as she slipped an arm out of the purple wool coat she had been wearing. She folded it over her arm and then passed it to her father. "Looks like everyone used your drop-off location instead," she said to Nick.

"Looks like," Nick agreed, his eyes squinting as he tried to figure her out. She wasn't offering much to work with. He placed the last jacket into the barrel, double checking to make sure the one he was left wearing belonged to him and wasn't meant for donation, too. He shoved his hands into his pockets and shrugged. "Aren't you going to be a little cold walking back to your shop without a jacket?"

Chrissy had been hugging her arms close to her body, but dropped them at his words. "Nope, I'm actually pretty warm most of the time. I'll be fine."

"Chrissy—you and I both know you're always freezing."

Out of his periphery, Nick could see a smirk form on Lee's mouth. "There are some things I need to tend to before I call it a night," Lee said. "Thank you both for bringing these by. I always love to see how generous our little town is this time of year. Brings me a lot of warmth."

"And hopefully all of these coats will do the same for those who need them," Nick said. "Grateful you've kept this tradition going all of these years."

"Me too, son. Me too." He walked over and shook Nick's hand and then turned and kissed the crown of his daughter's hair. "Love you, sweetie."

"Love you too, Dad."

Nick watched Chrissy and her dad say their good-byes and then he followed her out of the building. Even though they'd only been inside a few minutes, the skies had changed, light blue turning into a heavy, threatening gray. Wet, sloppy drops of snow pelted down like slushy rain around them.

"Here." Yanking his arm from his sleeve, Nick began to shrug out of his jacket.

"I'm not taking your jacket, Nick." Chrissy waved him off.

"Well, I'm not letting you walk back to your store in nothing but a thin shirt. You're going to catch a cold."

"I'll be fine."

Dropping his shoulders, Nick surrendered to her stubbornness, but only for a moment. He couldn't let her trudge through the town's square without a jacket. It was nearly freezing out. "If you won't take my coat, then at least share it with me."

Chrissy's eyes fell wide open. "Nick—"

"Come on." He kept one arm in its sleeve and held

out the other side of his jacket for Chrissy to slip into. It was a large pea coat with plenty of room for her to squeeze inside. "Just like we used to."

Water clung to her eyelashes and she blinked rapidly to see through them, the snow now sticking to every surface it touched. Nick could tell she didn't want to give in, but Mother Nature offered little alternative.

"Fine." She pressed her body to his as she huddled into the jacket.

Nick's throat tightened and he pulled in a steadying breath, trying to shake the nerves that came crashing in more fiercely than the storm that had shifted around them. White flurries cascaded over Spruce Street, making it a challenge to see. Luckily, they only had one short block to walk to the candle shop, but the white-out conditions didn't help them any.

"Who ordered this weather?" Nick teased as they quickened their stride, a difficult task with two people tucked into a single jacket. It was like competing in the potato sack race at Heirloom Point's Fourth of July Fair. They shimmied their way forward, but it was awkward and gangly and when Chrissy lost her footing, nearly slipping on the slick walkway, Nick grabbed onto her waist with his free hand to keep her from falling.

"Careful," he murmured.

She looked up at him, surprise in her gaze. "Thank you," she said in a voice hardly above a whisper.

"No problem." He smiled down at her and wondered if she could tell just how fast his heart raced. He was sure his pulse thrummed visibly in his neck.

They continued like that, waddling and wading through the angry weather until they reached her store.

Squeezing through the doorway as one unit, they toppled into the shop. If Nick hadn't known better, he would've thought they'd set foot in a bakery, all of the delectable smells making his mouth water.

"Gosh, Chrissy. It always smells so good in here."

Hurriedly, she slipped out of his jacket. He couldn't lie—he was a little disappointed that she wasn't pressed up against his side any longer, but the coat was sodden and wet, and keeping it on made him even colder. He pulled it from his body and hung it on a hook near the door to dry.

"I set the heater up in the backroom. You're welcome to warm up with me for a bit if you like."

It was an invitation Nick wasn't about to pass up. "Thank you. That would be great."

The store was dark, save for that Edison bulb that always shone dimly in the front display.

"How many years now?" Nick asked, nodding his head toward the old light.

"That bulb? Seventy-five years next week, actually."

"You'll never believe it, but when I was out in Washington for a game back in 2016, there was a celebration for a similar light bulb. It had been illuminated for a million hours at that point. They threw a party for it. A light bulb party. That bulb even had its own website." Nick chuckled as he recalled the memory. "Made me think of this one. Remember how we'd always stare at it from my parents' shop back in high school, just to see if it would flicker or go out? You said it was magic."

"I still think it must be. Sometimes magic is the only explanation."

"Sometimes it is." Nick looked at Chrissy, wanting to say more, but not knowing how. "Anyway. That space heater..."

"Right. Over here."

He followed Chrissy to a small workroom where bottles of oils were lined up, along with empty Mason jars ready to be filled with soy wax and wicks. There was even a small tabletop stove in the corner of the room. Nick figured Chrissy did most of her candle making in this portion of the shop and he was surprised by the overwhelming sense of pride that surged through him as he took it all in. Chrissy had become so successful, truly the Heart of Heirloom Point as evidenced by the many awards she'd received over the years with that exact title.

"Is this where the real magic happens?" he asked as he looked around.

"It's where the magic is supposed to happen, but this year it's like there's been some spell cast on me. I swear I cannot come up with anything for my holiday scent." Bending down, Chrissy plugged the heater into the wall and angled it their direction. Instantly, warm air rushed out. "If I don't create something soon, I'll have to go without a Christmas edition candle and I can't say people are going to be too happy about that."

"Let's brainstorm then."

"Nick, you don't have to help."

He pulled up a stool at the long workbench and motioned for Chrissy to take a seat on the one next to him. "I know I don't have to. I want to."

Conceding with a tentative smile, Chrissy scooted out the chair and lowered onto it. All the heat the space heater put out couldn't compare to the warmth of Chrissy so close to Nick, sitting side by side. At one point in time, he thought their entire lives would take place side by side. He couldn't dwell on that anymore. The past was the past. The future was unknown. But the present—this moment in the candle shop with Chrissy—this was a gift. He would treat it as such.

"So. How exactly do you do this? What's the first step in making a candle?"

"The actual candle making comes later. It's deciding what fragrances to use that has me stumped." Chrissy shook her head. "I feel like I've lost all of my creativity, you know? Do you ever feel that way? Like you just can't create?"

"I wouldn't say I have much creativity to lose to begin with," Nick said, jabbing her lightly with his elbow.

Sitting forward a bit in her seat, Chrissy reached for the bottles on the shelf. She selected a handful and placed them onto the table. "I think everyone has the ability to create. At least I used to. But I'm beginning to prove myself wrong."

"What is it that has you so stumped?" Like most men, Nick was a problem solver, and this was a challenge he wanted to help Chrissy overcome. It seemed simple enough.

"I can't seem to come up with anything new." She twisted the lid to a bottle labeled *cloves* and lifted the dropper to her nose, inhaling as her eyes shut. She opened them and then set the dropper back into its bottle. "I'm starting to wonder if there are only so many Christmas combinations out there when it comes to fragrances. I've already made candles that smell like trees. Others that smell like baked goods. Ones that evoke thoughts of winter and freshly fallen snow. Really, what's left? I think I've probably covered everything."

"Why do you think it's such a bad thing to repeat the past?" he challenged, no longer feeling like he was referring to the candles.

Her head whipped his direction, an apprehensive look on her face. "I don't think it's a bad thing," she replied with more grit in her tone than necessary. "I just worry what others will think."

Pressing closer, Nick dropped his gaze to her mouth fleetingly as he said, "And why do you care what others think?"

He could see her chin quiver, her lips trembling faintly. "I don't care what others think."

"Yes," he said soft and low, unable to keep from leaning closer. "You just said you worry what others will think."

"I don't care what they think," she repeated and this time the tremble found its way into her voice. Her eyes darted from Nick's down to his mouth and back up to his eyes where she searched him out, trying to read his intentions. "I really don't."

In the shelter of the backroom, with the storm pummeling the rooftop insistently overhead, Nick felt a magnetic pull toward Chrissy, like the energy from the flurry had merged its way into their beings, electric and powerful. She felt it, too; he could plainly see that. His breathing picked up in tempo, masked only in sound by the heater that whooshed back and forth over them.

Looking out from under her fringe of lashes, Chrissy pressed forward, closing the gap.

Nick lifted his hand and grazed her cheek delicately with his finger. He swept a lock of hair behind her ear and then cupped her jaw with his hand. Suddenly, he was fifteen again, that first kiss build-up and anticipation enough to make his head spin like he'd been riding a merry-go-round.

"Chrissy…" he swallowed, then leaned all the way forward, forgetting all the absent years, only caring about this moment in time with the only woman he had ever loved.

"Nick…"

CHRISSY

CHRISSY SHOT UP from the stool, the spark jerking her out of the trance she'd all-too-easily slipped into. She rushed toward the outlet and yanked the cord from the wall. The smell of electrical smoke in the air was so different from the kind her candles produced and it stung her nose and made her eyes water.

"What on earth happened?" She whirled around to face Nick. His hands were on his thighs and he shook his head like he had to collect himself and his thoughts before answering.

"Looks like maybe a tripped breaker," he hissed through his teeth.

"From the heater?"

"More than likely." He sighed and then stood. "Do you know where your breaker box is? I can check it out for you if you like."

"It's out in the front room. On the east wall, I think."

"Gotcha. I'll go take a look and see what's going on."

Chrissy was grateful for the temporary solitude. She needed a moment to herself to replay what might have happened had that outlet not popped so loudly, making her duck for cover.

She was about to kiss Nick.

Nick McHenry, her first boyfriend and ex-fiancé.

What in the world had gotten into her? Maybe it was the jacket. Snuggled up next to him, their bodies forced so intimately close, the pleasant, warm scent of his familiar cologne—it was like some portal had opened up and whisked her back in time.

She ran her fingers across her lips and briefly closed her eyes.

"Chrissy?" Nick called out from the other room. His tone held enough uncertainty that she knew her attention was needed elsewhere and not focused on old memories she had no business rerunning. "Can you come here for a second?"

When she rounded the corner, her heart bottomed out, like an anchor had been wrapped around it and thrown overboard.

Nick stood in the middle of the room, a light bulb in his hand.

"What—?" She nearly choked. "What happened?"

"It's out, Chrissy." His voice was gentle. "I'm so sorry."

"It's gone out before. Briefly, but it always comes back on." She tried to conceal the vibration in her voice. Rushing forward, she took the bulb from him. "We'll just screw it back in. I bet it will work if we just put it back."

"I already tried that." He took a step forward. "I'm so sorry."

"It's been on forever. I can't imagine a tripped breaker is enough to make it go out for good."

Nick's sincere demeanor didn't change as he came up behind her and placed a hand on the small of her back. "Maybe it was the storm. Who knows? But I don't think it's going to come back on, Chrissy. I don't think it has anything left. I'm sorry."

She shrugged like she didn't care about the light bulb as much as she did. "It's fine. It's just a light. Some things aren't meant to last forever."

Nick pulled back his hand. "Right. I guess that's true."

"I should get back to my candle making."

He looked at her like he'd been shocked with the same current that jolted the store moments earlier. "I'll just get my coat and head out."

"Thank you again for sharing it with me on the walk back."

"It's nothing, Chrissy."

She didn't want to read into his words. It hadn't felt like nothing. It felt like everything.

She also hoped he hadn't read into hers, the words that declared the end to things that at one point in time, felt like they could last forever, too.

❄

"IT'S ONLY A light bulb." Everleigh plopped down

next to Chrissy. She speared a piece of iceberg lettuce with her fork and brought the bite of salad to her mouth. "And honestly, considering that this is a candle shop, it shouldn't really make any difference whether or not that light is on. You have plenty of other resources to choose from."

"What Everleigh is saying is true," Nita offered, smiling sweetly as always, "but I do understand why you're disheartened, dearie. We're all just so used to seeing that old bulb on that it'll take some getting used to now that it's gone out. Change is always difficult."

"And sad," Chrissy added.

"Not always sad, sweetie." Nita took Chrissy by the shoulders and squeezed in a grandmotherly way. "Sometimes at first, but things get better with time. Trust me." Glancing around Chrissy, Nita surveyed the workbench. Sets of oils were grouped together, Chrissy's last five candle combinations lined up in order, year by year. "You doing something with these? A little holiday inspiration?"

"The opposite, actually. I got them out so I don't accidently replicate them in this year's blend."

Everleigh lifted a napkin to her mouth and wiped it, then said, "I think you might be going about this all wrong."

"Yeah? How so?"

"You're so stuck on not repeating the past that I think you're missing a big opportunity here."

Chrissy couldn't grasp her sister's point.

"Let's try something," Everleigh proposed, picking up the vanilla oil from the *Santa's Sugar Cookie* candle, the candied ginger from Chrissy's *Merry Mulled Christmas Cider,* pine needle from *Balsam and Bells,* spruce from *Winter Wreath,* and the peppermint oil from *Freshly Laden Snow.* She pulled out the droppers from each little bottle and wrapped her hands around them, bundling them like a bouquet of wildflowers. "Close your eyes."

Chrissy followed her sister's guidance and kept her eyelids shut as Everleigh waved the small syringes beneath her nose.

"Breathe in."

"I see what you're getting at." Pulling in a deep inhale, Chrissy trapped it in her lungs before blowing it out through her mouth. "Hmm, I actually like it. But something's off."

Nita leaned in and took a whiff. "I agree. Almost there, but not quite."

Flashing her eyes open, Chrissy reached over and snatched the sugar oil bottle from the table. "Swap out the peppermint with this."

The sisters traded droppers, then all three women pressed forward and breathed in.

Chrissy couldn't keep the massive grin from her face. "That's it!"

"Did I, or did I not, tell you that I would be the one to come up with this year's candle scent?" Everleigh boasted with a haughty laugh.

"You can't take all the credit," Nita said. "You took bits and pieces from Chrissy's previous blends. Like little memories from each candle."

"Christmas Memories!" Everleigh exclaimed. "Man, I am on fire! That's totally what you should call it."

"Christmas Memories?" Chrissy let the name roll around on her tongue, but she wasn't sure she loved the sound of it. It felt a little generic.

"Yes," Everleigh said. "It's the perfect name."

"Maybe not *perfect*." Leaning forward, Chrissy breathed in the pleasing combination of oils once more. "But I do love this. This blend, right here, is perfect."

"It's like an heirloom, all these pieces of nostalgia wrapped up in one scent," Nita said.

"An Heirloom Christmas," Chrissy agreed. "That, I *do* love."

Everleigh placed a hand on her sister's shoulder and grinned. "See? All you needed was a little help to find what was right there all along."

❄

CHRISSY TURNED THE note over in her hands, folding and unfolding it like a piece of origami. She didn't see it at first. When she went to lock up the store for the night, her heart sank at the apparent absence of a letter. She'd begun to anticipate them, hope for them, almost. Sure, she'd only received two so far, but it felt like there was some sort of meaning behind their placement in her wreath. Some purpose that she didn't quite yet grasp. She hadn't realized how much she wished for another piece to that puzzle.

Shoulders slouched, Chrissy shook off her disappointment as she slipped the key into the lock to secure the shop. Then, just as she turned to go, she caught a glimpse of something in her periphery. Looking closer, she spotted it amongst the foliage. The forest green color of the paper camouflaged it and it was stuffed deeper into the wreath than normal, wedged between the branches and the door. But it was still there.

Bounding and barreling down the hill—
It's always such a rush and thrill!
Pick your partner and secure your space
for the annual Heirloom Point Sledding Race!

Chrissy didn't need any sort of reminder for this event. As teenagers, she and Nick had competed as a team and each of those years resulted in first place trophies and frostbitten cheeks. In fact, they were a bit of a legend when it came to downhill sledding endeavors.

It wasn't just the competition that Chrissy loved. Unlike other run-of-the-mill sledding races, Heirloom Point's was practically a parade down the mountainside. Teams decorated and retrofitted their sleds to match the annual theme. This year's theme was Christmas carols. Chrissy already had a few ideas up her sleeve, but there was one thing she didn't have yet: a partner.

Everleigh had been her go-to teammate in recent races, but since her sister had accepted the position as president of this year's judging committee, it disqualified her from competing. That was almost enough to keep Chrissy from entering the race altogether. It wouldn't be the same skidding and sliding down the hill without Everleigh in tow.

Tightening her scarf around her neck and slipping her hands into her woolen gloves, Chrissy stuffed the note into her purse and walked to her car parked along the curb. She made a mental note to visit her favorite little clothing boutique the next day during her lunch break to purchase a new coat. How silly she had been that afternoon when she'd donated hers just so she didn't have to admit to Nick the real reason she was at the station. She supposed the note had prompted her visit as well, but once she saw him lumbering down the sidewalk looking like the Michelin Man, she needed very little in the way of prompting. She had to scope the hilarious scene out for herself.

Laughing under her breath at the memory, Chrissy reached for her key fob and was about to click open the lock when a dark SUV pulled up next to her, the thick tires crunching the snow underneath as it slowed to a stop in the middle of the street. Her interest piqued, she paused as the passenger door opened. She saw a boot meet the pavement first, then the large duffle bag that swung out from the vehicle before the passenger did.

Then, standing in front of her, broad and tall as a Ponderosa Pine, was Kevin McHenry, Nick's older brother and Chrissy's longtime friend.

"Chrissy!" Swooping headlong toward her, Kevin wrapped an arm around Chrissy and greeted her with a kiss on her cheek. He dropped his bag to the pavement in order to curl his other arm around her for a full, firm embrace. "I was hoping you'd be the first face I'd see when I got back into town!"

She didn't mean to blush at the statement, but the attention was endearing and Kevin had always been so good to her. It was nice to see him back in Heirloom Point, if only for the confirming knowledge that he was safe and out of harm's way. She knew he had some time off coming up with the Air Force, but Chrissy hadn't anticipated a holiday arrival. It was so good to see his friendly face.

"I didn't know you were coming home for Christmas, Kevin," she admitted as he settled her back onto solid ground.

"I didn't either until a few days ago. My mom is over the moon."

"I'm sure she is. Both of her boys home for the holidays. I bet she's cooking up your favorite meal as we speak."

Kevin beamed. "You know our family so well. Meatloaf and mashed potatoes are on tonight's menu. Lasagna for tomorrow."

"That meatloaf was always my favorite dish." Chrissy couldn't keep from salivating. Grace was the queen of comfort food and over the years, Chrissy had the privilege of partaking in that comfort around the McHenry dining table.

"I know it was. Except for the bits of carrot Mom sneaks into it. Don't pretend I didn't see you pick yours out and put them on Nick's plate back in the day."

"You saw that?" Chrissy's face warmed despite the

snowflakes that fluttered across it. She didn't like carrots, but had always been too shy to tell Grace. Criticizing a woman's cooking was never an acceptable thing to do, especially a woman who, at one point, was your soon-to-be mother-in-law.

"We all saw it, Chrissy. Can I let you in on a little secret?" Chrissy nodded, encouraging Kevin to continue. "Mom stopped putting carrots in her meatloaf years ago just in case you happened to come by for dinner again. Speaking of, it's cold and I'm hungry and if I'm guessing correctly, you're headed home without any dinner plans of your own."

"Why would you think that?"

"Because you put one-hundred percent into your candles, and if I remember right, it's the holiday candle making time of year. My bet is you didn't even eat lunch today."

"I had a granola bar around noon."

Kevin smirked. "You just proved my point. Come to Mom and Dad's for dinner, will you? Plus, I need a ride, so it's a win-win all around."

"Why didn't you just have your driver drop you off there?"

"That was the plan, but then I saw you and had to stop. It's been too long, Chrissy." Kevin went in for another hug, but this one felt different than the first. "Too long."

"I don't want to intrude," Chrissy said, half-hugging Kevin back. She knew at one point in time, the man had had feelings for her. He'd asked her out on more than one occasion, and had he been anyone other than Nick's brother, she probably would've accepted at least one of those persistent invitations. He was an undeniably handsome man with a huge heart and even bigger personality. That charisma was both charming and intriguing. Chrissy knew she shouldn't feel guilty that she had never reciprocated his affection and she hoped that an accepted dinner invitation wouldn't give him any false ideas or hopes this time around.

"Come on." Kevin detected her hesitation. "It's just dinner. You've got to eat."

"Alright," Chrissy conceded. "But if there are any carrots, I'm out of there," she teased.

Kevin laughed deeply. "Deal."

NICK

❄

"NICK, CAN YOU grab the candied carrots from the oven? They should be just about done."

Grace McHenry's kitchen smelled incredible. If good food could feel like a physical force, this was a hearty embrace. The perfectly browned buttermilk rolls were cooling on the counter, the meatloaf resting on a hot pad next to the stove, and there were fluffy, whipped potatoes scooped into a large serving bowl, ready to be dished onto plates in heaping spoonfuls.

A dinner like this could only mean one thing: Kevin was on his way home.

Nick was cautiously eager to see his brother. "What time will he be in?" he asked his dad, Joe, as he slipped his hands into two oven mitts and pulled on the oven door. Heat rushed out, flushing his face and singeing his eyelashes.

"Any minute. This afternoon's storm delayed his flight, but last I heard he landed an hour ago and then grabbed a ride on over." As his father spoke, the telltale creak of the unoiled front door hinges drew their attention away from the food and toward the entryway. "Speak of the devil."

"Kevin!" Grace threw off her apron and bounded for the foyer. "Kevin! You're home!"

Settling his rucksack onto the hardwood floor, Kevin raced toward his mother. "Mom!" he greeted as he scooped her up and twirled her around like part of a choreographed dance.

Kevin was Nick's big brother in every sense of the word: stature, personality, and in his uncanny ability to make a grand entrance.

With the steaming dish of carrots in his hands, Nick poked his head around the kitchen corner and nodded toward Kevin. "Hey there, Kev."

"Hey, little bro." Kevin strode over and balled up a fist to mess Nick's hair. "It's been a bit."

"Just a little." Nick shrugged back from his brother's roughhousing attempt. "Good to see you again."

"You, too."

Rushing back into the kitchen, Grace flapped her hands toward her youngest son and hissed under her breath, "Get rid of the carrots."

"What?" The dish was hot in Nick's hands. "Why would I get rid—"

"Look who I ran into on my way here!" Kevin stepped back and suddenly Chrissy came into view, standing in the archway that separated the kitchen from the living room.

The casserole dished fumbled from Nick's grip, clattering noisily onto the counter. "Chrissy?"

"Hi, everyone." She gave a timid wave and then clasped her hands in front of her body. "I'm so sorry to just show up like this."

"It's no problem at all, sweetheart. We're happy to have you. The more the merrier." As she said this, Grace took backward steps toward the counter, shielding the offending vegetable from Chrissy's view. Not-so-sneakily, Grace covered the dish with her discarded apron. "You always have a place at our table, I hope you know that."

"Thank you, Mrs. McHenry."

"Mrs. McHenry? Sweetheart, it always has been and always will be Grace with you."

Nick could interpret the relief in Chrissy's expression.

"Thank you, Grace. I appreciate it. Smells wonderful in here."

"Not quite as good as your candle shop," Grace said. "Everything's about ready if you boys want to get washed up for dinner. Chrissy, would you mind helping me set the table?"

"I'd be happy to."

While the women collected the utensils and cutlery, Nick joined his brother at the sink. He flipped the faucet on and spoke over the rush of water that tried to drown out his words. "What are you doing here with Chrissy?"

"I told you, I ran into her outside her shop on my way over." Kevin shoved his brother out of the way and pumped the soap dispenser. "She hadn't eaten yet, so I invited her to join us for dinner."

"Last I checked, the town's square is not on the way home from the airport."

"So I took a little detour?" Kevin shrugged. He pulled the towel from the counter and wiped his hands, then passed it to his brother so he could do the same. "We haven't seen each other in ten years and the first thing you want to do is quiz me about my driving route?"

"That's not what I want to quiz you about," Nick started in, but he was interrupted by his mother's beckoning from the dining room.

"Boys, we're waiting!"

"We can discuss this later, little bro. Right now my stomach is growling louder than you're talking."

Nick followed Kevin out of the kitchen and took a seat in between Chrissy and his father. The table was set with crimson placemats, napkins embroidered with metallic snowflakes, and tumblers boasting green and red plaid rims. In the center was an elegant vase of red and white roses with pine cones and needled ferns folded into the arrangement. Grace's dining table was always a welcoming sight, but during the holidays it was a festive masterpiece.

Like she couldn't hold it in any longer, Grace let out a squeal of excitement. "Goodness! I just can't believe this. Everyone here in one place, at Christmastime, no less!" She took her knife and fork into her hands and declared, "Let's eat!"

Dishes traded hands and utensils clanged as the

family partook in the spread before them. Kevin shared what he could about his most recent assignment, but there was always a bit of confidentiality involved in his life that made delving in too deep off limits. Even still, he could find plenty to fill the silent gaps that inevitably arose and Grace and Joe hung on their eldest son's words with rapt attention.

Glancing next to him, Nick noticed Chrissy push her food around her plate with the tines of her fork. She'd look up and smile as the conversation warbled around her, but there was a void, blank glaze over her eyes and an empty smile worn on her mouth, like she was there in presence only.

"She doesn't put carrots in it anymore," Nick whispered while Kevin recapped his turbulent plane ride, complete with swooping, charade-like arm movements. "It's totally safe."

"Oh." She settled her fork onto the tablecloth and grinned, this one with a hint of feeling. "That's not it. I guess I'm just not all that hungry."

"No worries. Mom's not going to be offended if you don't eat, Chrissy."

"I know she won't be." She looked over at Nick. "I think we should talk about what happened this afternoon," she spoke in a low volume with her head bent like she could trap the words there, keeping them tucked just between the two.

"Nothing happened." Nick shrugged and filled his mouth with a bite of potatoes. "We're good, Chrissy."

"You sure?"

"Yep. Totally sure."

Dinner became less about eating and more about Kevin retelling old stories Nick had heard so many times he could recite them by heart, and he hadn't even been the subject of them. Still, it was good to all be in one place again, if only to see the joy on his mother's face and hear the delight in his dad's robust laugh.

This was the reason Nick had come home, anyway. To be a part of a family again.

"Who's your partner this year, little bro?" Kevin's question was directed at Nick and it snapped him out of his wandering reverie. "For the sledding competition this weekend?"

"I haven't thought—"

"I am," Chrissy interjected. "We're a team."

Nick's eyes rounded in surprise, along with everyone else's at the table. "Oh, um..."

"Wow." Kevin pulled his chin to his chest. "Just like old times then, huh?"

"Yep." Chrissy nodded confidently as she continued, "We've been working on our sled for some time now. Wait until you see it. It'll blow all the other competition out of the water. Or rather, out of the snow."

Nick didn't know how to respond so he let Chrissy continue all on her own.

Kevin appeared confused. "Sounds like I've got to find myself a teammate soon or I'll be left in your dust."

"Left in our powder is what I think you mean."

"Oh, it's on!" Kevin clamped his hands down onto

the tabletop. "Dad? You in? Wanna race down the slopes against these two amateurs?"

"I don't know, son." Joe vacillated.

"It'll be fun, Joseph," Grace encouraged, tapping her husband's hand. "You haven't sledded in years."

"My point exactly."

"What could go wrong?"

"I could gravely injure myself and never be the same again."

Nick pushed back from the table and stood, then began collecting dishes, readying to take them to the kitchen to wash. "Speaking as someone who has done exactly that, I'm with Dad. Might be best if we both sit this year out."

In one swift motion, Chrissy scooted out her chair and trailed Nick, several more dinner plates in her hands.

"Nick," she called out from behind as she quickened her strides to catch up.

In the kitchen, Nick placed the stopper into the bottom of the sink and flipped the faucet to fill it with warm, sudsy water. After scraping the remaining bits of food into a nearby trash can, he placed the dishes into the basin.

"Nick," she said again as she settled her stack of plates onto the tile next to him. "I'm sorry. I don't know why I did that back there. We don't need to be partners. I didn't even think about your knee. Forget I ever mentioned it."

"It's fine, Chrissy." With the brush in hand, Nick began washing each plate. He scrubbed harder than necessary. He wasn't angry, but frustration bubbled within him and he needed a release.

Chrissy handed him a plate. "You wash, I dry?"

"Sure thing."

She scooted around to his right side and opened the top drawer containing clean dishrags. That Chrissy still knew where everything belonged within the McHenry household made Nick equal parts happy and sad. He couldn't figure out this space they'd created—this limbo of unacknowledged emotion.

"Honestly, I think my knee would be just fine," Nick admitted as he pulled the cleaned plate from the water and passed it to Chrissy. "I'm not sure my heart would be, though."

As she took the dish, Chrissy's hand brushed Nick's and those sparks from earlier ignited in his stomach, like a brilliant firework display. This woman still had such a hold on him, a hold he had no right to any longer.

"Nick..."

"I don't know what I'm doing here, Chrissy. In Heirloom Point. With you. I don't know what I'm supposed to be doing."

She looked down at the flour sack towel as she wiped the face of the plate. "I'm so sorry about your injury, Nick. If it had never happened, you'd still be living out your dreams on the road, making a name and a life for yourself."

"I'm not so sure."

"What do you mean?"

He pulled another plate from the now murky water

and handed it off. "I loved hockey, don't get me wrong. But it never loved me back. When it all comes down to it, it seems so silly to give that much devotion to something incapable of returning it."

Chrissy laid the plate silently onto the counter and turned to face him, empathy reflective in her blue eyes. "Nick, for what it's worth, I don't think you made the wrong decision in leaving. I think if you never pursued hockey, you'd always be left wondering what could have been."

"Funny, but that's exactly how I feel in this very moment. But not about hockey."

This time, when she reached for another plate, Chrissy dipped her hand into the water. Nick startled when her slender fingers found his, interlocking one by one until they were grasped tightly underneath the suds and bubbles. His heart rocketed into a faster beat. With his thumb, he lightly brushed over the back of her hand, cherishing how soft and familiar it felt, even with the water surrounding it.

"Got some more dishes that need washing!" Grace bellowed as she scurried into the kitchen.

Nick released Chrissy's hand so quickly it caused the dishwater to slosh up and over the sink rim, sending droplets scattering onto the tile, the kitchen window and the cabinets.

"Thanks, Mom," Nick sputtered. He cleared his throat with a quick cough. "We'll get those cleaned up."

Like she could sense she'd interrupted something meaningful, Grace tilted her head as she crept closer.

"Everything okay in here?" she pried in the way she'd perfected over the many years of motherhood.

"Yes, everything's fine, Mrs. McHenry." Chrissy folded and unfolded the dishrag, then shoved her hair from her face and plastered on a confident smile. "We'll get these washed right away."

"Take your time," Grace said as she walked out of the room in unhurried, backward steps, still sizing up the situation she'd stumbled upon. She nodded, then added with a knowing smirk, "Take all the time you two need."

CHRISSY

THEY HAD TEXTED back and forth all evening, and every time her phone dinged, Chrissy would jump, startled by the alert. They didn't have cell phones when they had dated as teenagers, only sharing notes during passing periods and in classes when they assumed their teachers' eyes were averted. Texting was new and the earnest excitement coupled with it was just as foreign.

Nick: *I'm glad Kevin brought you home to join us for dinner tonight. And I apologize again for the carrots. You weren't meant to see those. ;)*

Chrissy: *I still think it's silly that you didn't even serve them. You don't have to accommodate my picky eating habits.*

Nick: *Mom never wants anyone to be uncomfortable. She takes pride in her home being a welcoming place.*

Chrissy: *It has always felt so welcoming to me. Now, if I could only make my home feel the same.*

Chrissy cozied up with a mug of cider and a book again, a second attempt at the previously unsuccessful night of planned relaxation. Unfortunately, she was met with the same outcome. She picked the book up in between exchanged texts, but her attention remained concentrated on her phone and not the story unfolding on the pages.

Nick: *I'm sure your home is very welcoming, Chrissy. I can't imagine it being anything but.*

Chrissy: *The half-decorated Christmas tree screams otherwise.*

Chrissy glowered at the bleak tree before her. The cranberry garland was lovely, and the flocking was just her taste, but the lack of ornaments made its presence feel generic, like it was a department store tree and not one meant to bring warmth and cheer to a lived-in home.

Nick: *You know what would solve that?*

Chrissy: *What's that?*

Nick: *More decorations. Come on, Chrissy, I thought that was a given. Too easy.*

Snickering, Chrissy smiled to herself. She had always adored Nick's wit and the silly jokes and puns he effortlessly bantered.

Nick: *I made a batch of those salt dough ornaments if you'd like a few. Doris gave me a recipe and I didn't realize it was doubled. My Charlie Brown tree can't even hold them all. Want me to bring some by?*

Chrissy gasped. She was already in her yoga pants and sweatshirt with her hair in a messy topknot. She certainly wasn't suited for a night of entertaining.

Chrissy: *Right now?*

Nick: *If you're not busy. Plus, I'd really like to see the old Miller place. I won't stay long.*

Chrissy: *Sure.*

That works, she began to type, but quickly deleted the text, realizing it wasn't the most inviting reply.

Chrissy: *I'd like that.*

Nick: *Great. I'll be by in ten.*

That wasn't enough time to throw her home into a presentable state, so Chrissy decided to leave it be. There were dirtied dishes accumulating in the sink, but she'd done her share of dishwashing that evening. They could wait until morning.

Taking in her plain reflection in the hall mirror, she pulled in a sharp breath and opened the door when Nick arrived within ten minutes just as he stated he would.

"Hey there, Chrissy." He smiled sweetly at her like they hadn't already spent the good majority of the day together. "I come bearing gifts."

The tray of dough ornaments looked like something collected from a kindergarten classroom. Chrissy's heart squeezed at the endearing sight. "You made these?"

"I did," he boasted. "I know they're not the most attractive things, but you said you needed decorations, and I think they'll do a sufficient job." He looked around her and into the home. "Wow, Chrissy. This place is amazing."

"I should hope so, after all the blood, sweat, and tears I've put into it."

"I hope not literally," Nick said.

"Yes, literally. And money. A bit of that, too." Chrissy took the plate from Nick and placed it onto the side table in the foyer. "Would you like the official tour?"

"Absolutely. I thought you'd never ask."

They spent the next half hour meandering the Victorian home, room by room. Chrissy pointed out all of the notable additions and repairs she'd made to each area, mentioning the historical aspects she had tried to preserve during the renovation. Awe painted Nick's face, deepening with every square foot of the house they covered.

Chrissy wondered what thoughts filled his head—if he placed himself into the home and its story the way she knew he had once before. There was something hidden—trapped, almost—behind Nick's hazel gaze that she couldn't decipher, no matter how intently she studied him.

That inability made her insecure with doubt. Had she done the house justice? Were the changes she'd made for the better? Or had some of the home's historical integrity been lost in the fresh layers of paint, in the new trims and repairs moldings? There was a hope for approval that she didn't know she needed, and it left her wordless with worry.

They ended the tour at the base of the Christmas tree, admittedly, a humdrum finish.

"I wouldn't change a thing," Nick said, finally.

Chrissy eased out the relieved breath she'd been harboring deep in her lungs. "Really?"

"Well, maybe one thing."

"And what's that?"

"This tree. It really could use some more ornaments. It's only half-decorated."

Chrissy couldn't keep the roll from her eyes. "Well, it's a good thing I know just where I can find some." Quickly, she retrieved the plate she'd stowed in the entryway. She hadn't looked at them thoroughly when Nick handed them off earlier, and she was grateful he was tucked away in another room now when she gave them a closer inspection.

They were absolutely hideous.

Nick hadn't been exaggerating back at the candle shop—he really didn't have much in the way of creativity.

She tried to silence the snicker that threatened to sputter out, but masking it took an effort she couldn't muster.

"You made all of these?" she asked, hiding her giggle behind a cupped hand.

"Sure did." Pride pulled at the corners of Nick's lips.

"They're..."

"You don't like them."

"No, no. It's not that I don't like them."

"It's okay, Chrissy. You don't have to like them. You already know that I don't like the flocking," he said with a shrug. "I don't think these particular ornaments could possibly make it look any worse."

"Nick McHenry!" Smacking his solid chest with her hand, Chrissy sneered. "The flocking is beautiful!"

"That's your opinion," he teased, readied for another friendly swat that didn't come. "And I think these ornaments are miniature works of art. My opinion."

Selecting a particularly misshapen looking snowman from the tray, Chrissy held it up at eye level between them. "This is a work of art?"

"It's Slushy!"

"You mean Frosty," she corrected.

"No. I mean Slushy, the snowman Dad and I used to build outside the store. Frosty's much hipper, trendier cousin." Nick snatched the ornament from her hands. "You don't think it looks like him?"

"Oh my gosh! I forgot about that snowman. You know, your dad hasn't built it since you left."

"Well, we have big plans to bring Ol' Slushy out of retirement this year, so be on the lookout for his impending debut."

"I'm eagerly awaiting it."

Chrissy hung the disproportionate snowman on the tree and reached for another ornament to place on the barren branches. There were cutout gingerbread men and snowflakes and presents and cocoa mugs, each one less impressive than the last. Still, Chrissy took comfort in their homemade appearance. Nick wasn't ever what she would consider crafty. She remembered back to art class their junior year, when Mrs. Gemma had asked her students to draw self portraits to place on display at Back to School Night. Nick's was an honest-to-goodness stick figure. It wasn't that he hadn't tried; that stick figure was impressively accessorized with hockey gear from his helmet down to the puck and skates. But the fact of the matter remained: Nick would never be a gifted artist or renowned illustrator. Most of his talents were of the athletic variety which was nothing to scoff at.

As she gathered each ornament, readying to fill her tree with his mediocre creations, Chrissy felt what she imagined a parent might feel when receiving a handmade birthday card or gift. She saw through the end product and into the heart of it. She saw Nick standing at his oven, impatiently opening and closing the door as he waited for the decorations to bake. She saw him seated at his kitchen table, brushing layers of paint onto the ornaments to bring them to life. She saw him stringing the red yarn through the holes to create a hook made for displaying.

She saw all of these things and without intending to, she pictured herself right there with him.

"Penny for your thoughts?" Nick asked after a long stretch of quiet. They'd covered a quarter of the tree, but still, it looked underdressed.

"I was just imagining you making all of these. I'm sure it took a lot of time—I almost feel bad for teasing you about them now."

"You shouldn't feel bad; you should feel relieved. Remember, long ago we had plans to create something on a much larger scale." He looked around the living room to indicate his meaning. "You should be grateful I wasn't involved in any of this, Chrissy. If these ornaments are any marker of my abilities, I would have completely ruined this house."

"Well, I don't think these ornaments *are* any indicator. Baking Christmas tree decorations and rebuilding a home are certainly not one and the same. And as I remember, construction is something you actually *do* excel at. You've been known to construct a champion sled or two in your day."

"I suppose you're right about that. We did make some winning sleds, didn't we?"

"Absolutely. They even had a name for us, remember?"

"The Dashing Duo." Nick beamed a broad grin that burst onto his face. "Because we looked so incredibly dashing as we raced down the slopes."

"I think it had to do a little more with the Jingle Bells song lyrics *dashing through the snow.*"

"Believe what you will."

Chrissy liked this, the ability to be with Nick and not feel pressured to have any sort of label or status. Over the next hour, they continued placing the ornaments on the tree. Conversation grew easily between them. Every once in a while Nick would ask a question about the remodel which propelled them into discussions about permits or plans. It was as though they both fought to stay at the surface level, not wishing to carve too deep into each other's lives by asking the questions they truly wanted answered.

Even though she felt like she should be, Chrissy wasn't entirely satisfied with that. For now, she would have to be.

When the last of the ornaments were settled onto the branches, they both stepped back, arms crossed over their bodies, heads tilted in examination.

"Still missing something."

"A tree topper!" Chrissy blurted as her gaze traveled up the tree to the empty point.

"Do you happen to have one?"

"Nope."

Nick lowered his head and snickered a laugh under his breath. "I gotta admit, Chrissy—you're not the most prepared when it comes to Christmas tree decorating."

"I've had a lot on my mind this season," she said. "There is a box I got down from the attic earlier today that has some leftover decorations. Maybe we can find something in there?"

"Worth a shot."

They sifted through the tub which contained the sorts of holiday items one should part with. Still, Chrissy hung onto them for no apparent reason. Packages of half-used greeting cards, a nutcracker missing his lever, a snow globe with a leak, and an already opened Advent calendar, just to name a few.

"This is quite the box of mismatched Christmas décor, Chrissy."

"I have a hard time parting with things," she admitted as she pulled out an old Santa hat and shoved it onto Nick's head, all the way down over his eyebrows.

He peeked out from under the white fur trim. "Ho, ho, ho," he bellowed, shoulders bouncing jollily like the Man in Red himself. "This isn't the hat you stole from Santa, is it?"

"I didn't steal it."

"Um, yes, you did. If I remember, that Santa said you were too old to make a wish and you snatched the hat from his head and took off running. It took me two full blocks before I was able to catch up with you. Man, you were fast."

"I had to prove that he wasn't the real Santa. I was certain all that white hair was just a wig. Who tells a kid they're too old to make a Christmas wish, anyway? Certainly not the official Mr. Claus."

"You weren't really a kid, Chrissy. You were sixteen."

"I don't know—that feels like a kid to me. Sometimes I still feel like that girl, you know?"

"The one who wants so badly to believe in Santa?" Nick swiped the hat from his head and examined it, turning it over in his hands as he recalled the memory.

"No, the one who wants so badly to believe in magic. And that's what Santa represents, I suppose—the magic of Christmas wishes granted and made true."

"Well, I, for one, think it's pretty magical that you held onto this Santa hat all these years. It's like you knew we would need it tonight."

"What do we need an old Santa hat for?"

"The tree topper, of course!" Nick rose from his seated position on the hardwood floor.

Chrissy saw him wince, a flare of pain pulling his features tight. She stood up, too. "You okay?"

"Yup," he said through clamped teeth. He stretched and flung the hat onto the tallest branch. "There. Perfect finishing touch."

Then, like his leg completely gave way, Nick faltered, tumbling headfirst toward Chrissy. Instinctually, she shot out her arms to wrap around his waist, propping him against her body to keep them both securely upright and not sprawled out underneath the tree.

"Whoa, there," she uttered. They were so close she could feel his breath on her lips, feel the rise and fall of his chest. "Careful."

Startling her, Nick began to chuckle, quietly at first, just his shoulders lifting up and dropping down without audible sound. But his laugh steadily grew, to the point and volume that Chrissy couldn't keep herself from joining in.

"What are we laughing at?" she asked in between fits of giggles.

"This isn't the way it usually goes," he said. His whole body shook with unbidden laughter now. "In the movies, it's always the woman falling off a ladder into the man's arms. Not a clumsy guy almost squishing the beautiful girl while he's still on solid ground."

"You didn't almost squish me," she said, her eyes examining his. She parted her lips.

Nick pulled away. He rubbed the back of his neck and then focused his gaze on the floor. "I should go."

"You don't have to."

"No, I do," he said, his eyes lifting up to meet hers. "I think this is as good as this tree is going to look without some professional intervention. I just hope my contributions didn't make it worse."

"I think it's perfect, Nick."

"That's awfully generous," he teased. "Anyway. I'll see you tomorrow?"

"Sure. Yeah."

They walked to the door, Chrissy trailing behind Nick, fumbling for something to say to button up their evening. It felt like it had unexpectedly unraveled within the matter of minutes.

"Goodnight, Chrissy."

"Night, Nick."

He had his hand on the door handle when he hesitated. Then, whirling around, he gathered Chrissy up into his arms and hugged her like his very life depended on it.

Chrissy was familiar with that sort of hug.

It was just like the last one he'd given her when he left Heirloom Point the first time.

NICK

IT SNOWED FOR the next three days with little promise of reprieve. Nick didn't need the sunshine to ensure a good mood, but by the fourth day of a constant covering of gray, his thoughts started to bend in that gloomy direction, too.

Kevin and Joe had hunkered down with their sled blueprints, making it abundantly clear that they had no plans to unveil their project until the competition. It was top-secret sort of work. Luckily, the sledding race was scheduled for the following day. Nick couldn't lie; he was growing increasingly interested in their sledding plans.

The more he watched their excitement develop over the small-town tradition, the more Nick felt guilty that he'd shot down Chrissy's partnership offer so quickly. They always had made a good team. He knew she'd said it in passing, mostly as a response to Kevin's probing questions. Even still, he caught the hint of hope in Chrissy's words and eyes. He wondered if that hope remained or if it had dwindled completely as the competition grew closer.

Nick woke up early that morning with big plans and an even bigger craving for a peppermint latte. That was certainly a first. Something about decorating Chrissy's tree felt like an ushering in of the holiday season. Apparently even his taste buds were ready to celebrate. He watched several online video tutorials until he was confident he had a handle on the intimidating espresso machine which still sat untouched on the counter.

It wasn't nearly as difficult as he thought it would be. He only had to discard three beverages before arriving at one that actually wasn't half bad. By his fourth try, he felt like even Doris would be proud.

With two travel mugs in hand, Nick locked up the house and headed up the path toward Lee's home. The streets were newly plowed, charcoal-colored snow pressed up against the curbs like slushy barricades. Heavy snowflakes flurried around, leaving Nick's cheeks wet where they landed. He knew his nose reddened with each cold drop.

Rounding the walkway, Nick noticed Audrey's wreath still hanging on the door. At least this time Nick wasn't showing up unannounced. In fact, despite the chilly temperatures, Lee was already waiting, rocking back and forth on a chair. He tossed a wave into the air.

"Mornin', Nick!" he hollered from the porch.

"Good morning, Lee. I brought you a peppermint latte. I can't promise it's any good, but I think it's probably drinkable."

"Anything's better than the coffee we've got down at that station. Can't say I've ever seen anyone clean that carafe with anything more than just a quick rinse under the faucet. That coffee—that's the kind that will put hair on your chest." Lee took the mug from Nick after he ascended the steps to the house. He drew in a first sip. "This," he swallowed, "well this coffee right here just might turn you into a Christmas elf!"

Nick snorted a laugh. "I felt extra Christmassy this morning. I even threw a candy cane in there."

"You don't say?" Lee replied, sarcasm generous in his tone. He took another drink and coughed. "What's gotten you in this particularly seasonal mood, son?"

"Just being back home, I think. Remembering old traditions and making new ones."

"Speaking of, I found the thing you called about last night. It's over in the garage. Let's take a look, shall we?"

Lee's detached garage was just a few paces from the house. He'd never used it to store a vehicle, instead using it as a workshop of sorts. Lee pressed his shoulder into the stubborn door and it gave way on its hinges. The scent of wood shavings and oil and must hit Nick's senses.

"Right this way." Stepping around several fruit crates and an old table saw, Lee created a narrow path through the cluttered odds and ends.

There was a sheet-covered mound on a workbench and, like he was a magician, Lee grabbed the corner and yanked it off in one theatrical swoop. "Ta-da!" he bellowed. "Truth be told, I'm surprised I still had this old thing. Audrey asked me to clean out this shed more times than I can count, but I never seemed to get around to it. Now I don't feel so bad about that. This is practically an antique."

Nick walked around the table, surveying the sled from all angles. It was laden with dust, which was to be expected after so many years of not being used. A coat of paint would freshen it up and have it looking good as new in no time. He peered closer, looking for the notches in the pine that he hoped were still detectable. Just where he remembered carving them, four lines remained scratched deeply into the sled's surface.

"Four-time champions," Lee said, looking over Nick's shoulder at the carvings. "That's nothing to sneeze at."

"I'm hoping to make it five."

"You got any ideas for this year? I hear the theme has something to do with Christmas carols. In fact, I've got an old refrigerator box that you're welcome to use to construct your sled. Although you probably have several shipping boxes of your own from the recent move."

"I've yet to ship out the rest of my belongings, so I'll definitely take you up on that box. I'll also take you up on a little help if you're willing to offer that, too."

Lee beamed. "Son, I thought you'd never ask."

❄

IT DIDN'T TAKE long to construct the sled. Nick was grateful not only for Lee's help, but for his creative eye, something Nick admittedly lacked. He had a vision for the *Jingle Bells*-themed sled, but translating that idea from his head into reality was met with great difficulty. Luckily, Lee caught onto Nick's concept quickly and before the morning was over, they had an impressive one horse open sleigh equipped with Chrissy's childhood stick horse at the helm, silver bells strung across the red cardboard sides, and a spray painted snow finish to top it all off.

Nick couldn't wait to take it down the slopes.

"If the winner is chosen based on looks alone, this sled will surely win you the title," Lee said, admiring their final product as he appreciatively stroked his moustache.

"That's only half of it. We need to hope this thing is more aerodynamic than it looks. It's a bit clunky, isn't it?"

"I think it will do just fine. They're all clunky, home-made contraptions. That's just the nature of the beast. So, when do you plan to show Chrissy?"

"Right now. That is, if you can help me load it into the back of the truck." Nick peered through the garage window out at the street and the suddenly clearer skies. "Looks like the snow's even let up for a bit."

"I think we shouldn't waste any time then. To the truck we go!"

❄

JUST AS HE had hoped, Chrissy was working at her candle shop, her sedan parked right outside the storefront along the curb. Nick wasn't sure how to go about the whole thing. Should he formally ask her to be his sledding partner, unveiling the sled in some dramatic fashion as though asking her to a school dance? Or should he just mention it in passing, and, if she showed interest, show her the sled he'd spent the entire morning crafting with her father?

Nick didn't have much time to equivocate because Chrissy suddenly came barreling out of the store, her face downward, focused intently on a piece of paper in her hands. Her eyes were narrowed and her mouth pinched tight.

"Chrissy?" Nick attempted to summon her attention.

Her gaze shot up to his. Instantly, her features relaxed. "Nick! What are you doing here?" And then her eyes traveled the path of Nick's, landing on the ornate sled perched in the bed of his truck. "Is that...?"

"Chrissy, would you care to be my partner for the sledding race tomorrow?" Apparently he was going the prom-posal route.

"Jingle Bells?" Her eyes were saucer wide. "Is that a Jingle Bells theme?"

"It is. I'm glad it's obvious. I was a little worried it didn't translate well. But I figured since we were once the Dashing Duo, it was only fitting." He forced a smile that trembled each time he tried it out on his lips.

"Nick, I..." She paused and then her face returned to the tight, concerned look she wore when she came out of the shop moments earlier.

"It's no big deal if you don't want to, Chrissy," he began backpedaling. "Your dad and I just whipped this up. It's totally fine if you don't want to be partners for the race. I should've asked first."

"Dad worked on this with you?"

"He did. In fact, all of the creative stuff is his doing. I just chose the carol."

Chrissy walked over to the sled. "My dad had the idea to use that stick horse?"

"That was me, actually."

"And he thought to string all of these jingle bells along the edges for the trim?"

"Well, that was me, too."

Chrissy nodded. "And the painted snow?"

"I do know how much you love fake snow." Nick smiled hesitantly. He couldn't decipher her reaction and it had his head spinning with doubt.

"This is one of the most thoughtful things anyone has done for me lately, Nick."

"It's really not all that thoughtful. It's just a cardboard-covered sled."

"It's more than that. The other night at dinner, I saw how uncomfortable it made you when I suggested we compete in this year's race together. And I get that. It's been a long time. But you put all of that aside and created this beautiful sleigh just for me. That means a lot to me, Nick."

"You mean a lot to me, Chrissy." He could see her eyes briefly expand in surprise before she composed her expression. "And winning title number five means a lot to me, too," he tacked on, hoping to avoid coming off too strong.

"Then I say we get signed up to take this puppy on the slopes tomorrow. I, for one, am eager to reclaim our rightful place on the podium. You know, Doris and Nita currently hold the title."

"I'm eager for that, too," Nick agreed, but that was just one title he hoped to reclaim when it came to Chrissy.

CHRISSY

CHRISSY PULLED THE slip of paper from her nightstand, though she didn't need to read it again to recall its wording. This one she had easily memorized.

> *Gowns and tuxedos*
> *A night of dancing for all*
> *You're formally invited to the*
> *Heirloom Point Winter Ball*

She set the note on her pillow. Rubbing the sleep from her eyes, she yawned and stretched, pushing down her thick comforter into a fabric accordion at the foot of her bed. A slice of winter sun slipped through the small opening in the drapes on her window and it painted the room with a strip of radiant light. Chrissy could feel the warmth on her cheeks and while she credited it to the morning sunlight, she also suspected it might have a little something to do with the invitation.

Chrissy hadn't been to a dance since prom, even though Heirloom Point hosted a ball each winter season. She'd always found an excuse not to attend. One year it was a root canal. The next it was a sprained ankle. Last year she happened to conveniently come down with a twenty-four-hour stomach bug.

This year, she had no real reason not to go. Even still, the thought of setting foot on a dance floor gave her jitters. Maybe Nick wouldn't even be in attendance, but she doubted that. If she had suspected the notes had been his doing before, this most recent one just solidified that hunch. It was obvious Nick had been going out of his way to mend their broken past, from his peace offering salt dough ornaments to the surprise *Jingle Bells* sled. Chrissy felt like she was starting to successfully interpret his intentions and there was an immense sense of relief in that.

She was eager to set out for Sugarcrest Hill, and readied herself for the day quickly, especially since she'd overslept. A light snow had fallen throughout the previous night, but let up just before dawn. That left a beautiful, fluffy dusting all across the town. Perfect conditions for a sledding race.

After eating a breakfast of toaster waffles and a banana, Chrissy laced her snow boots onto her feet and slung her newly purchased down jacket over her shoulders. Even though the snow no longer fell, it would still be cold on the slopes, the wind whipping with force as their sled careened down the hillside.

Nick had texted an hour earlier to let her know he'd

already driven by to check out the course. He said he even saw a few competitors taking a practice run down the mountain. While Chrissy figured that might be a good idea for their team, too, she wasn't sure she'd be able to make it there in time. Everleigh had told her that they would close the course a half-hour before the race was set to begin, and a quick glance at the clock let Chrissy know she only had ten minutes until that designated time.

She tried to hurry to the event location, but the streets she needed to drive hadn't yet been plowed and she really didn't want to slip and slide her way through town. She took her time, safety of the utmost importance. As she suspected, when she finally pulled into the lot, she could see Everleigh, megaphone in hand, calling the entrants in from the hill.

"Competitors, off the slopes!" she shouted. "Off the slopes!" She turned toward Chrissy who had exited her vehicle and walked over. "Hey, sis!" Everleigh screamed, her voice still echoing through the megaphone. Chrissy cringed. "Sorry." Everleigh released the button on the handle. "Hey, sis," she repeated, this time at a reasonable volume. "I just saw Nick with your sled. I didn't realize you two were competing together this year."

"I didn't either. It was sort of a last minute decision."

"The LOL's are quaking in their orthopedic boots. They figured they were a shoe-in until they saw the Dashing Duo listed on this year's entrant's form. I'm supposed to be impartial, but I secretly hope that sled of yours is faster than it looks. It would be nice to humble Doris a bit."

"She's nothing if not confident."

"And bossy," Everleigh added. "Rumor has it she was out here last night measuring the course and evidently it's two feet shorter than last year's. She had a mini fit over that. I had to restring all the boundary lines and reset the markers before sunup. I tell you, for a volunteer position, this is really demanding. Anyway, go find Nick. You missed your chance for a practice run, but you still have time to work on some last-minute strategies."

"Sounds good. See you in a bit, sis."

"See ya."

The base of the mountain was filled with racers, each sledding team paired off as they huddled around their designs. Some themes were easily recognizable, like *Rudolph the Red-Nosed Reindeer* and *Frosty the Snowman* with their respective characters painted on the sides in cartoon-like drawings. Other sleds took a bit of creative interpretation. Chrissy stared at Tucker and Marcie's sleigh for a long while before it finally clicked. Their sled had varying strips of cloth tacked to the sides, all in shades of green.

"Greensleeves," Chrissy said appreciatively as she stepped toward her friends. "I like it."

"I'm so glad you get it," Tucker said. "Over twenty t-shirts and sweaters sacrificed their lives for this silly sled. My entire wardrobe became sleeveless overnight. I sure hope male tank-tops are making a comeback, because that's all I currently have in my closet."

"Um, yeah, I sincerely doubt that will happen," Marcie said with a roll of her eyes. "Chrissy, I just saw

Nick with your sled. It's amazing! Jingle bells, jingle bells, jingle all the way!"

"I wish I could take credit, but that's all Nick's doing."

"Either way, it's totally awesome. Almost as good as those little old ladies."

"Really? Theirs is that good, huh?" Chrissy glanced around. "I haven't seen it yet."

"Oh, you have to go check it out. They brought their A-game, for sure." Marcie slugged her brother in the shoulder. "Come on, Tuck. Let's jump back in this sled and practice our maneuvers." She gave Chrissy a look that indicated annoyance with Tucker. "I swear, this brother of mine doesn't know his right from his left. I tell him to lean one way and he goes the other. It'll be a miracle if we can even keep this thing within the course boundaries. I bet we end up disqualified when all is said and done."

Chrissy laughed. "I'll leave you two to work that out."

"Alrighty, friend. See you on the slopes!"

Each look at the sleds had Chrissy humming a different holiday tune. There was *Little Drummer Boy* and *Rockin' Around the Christmas Tree* with their musical notes and instruments incorporated into the design scheme. Others were more traditional carols like *Silent Night* and *White Christmas*. Then, a few yards up, she saw Kevin and Joe, each with a hammer poised in hand, making final changes to their toboggan.

"Wow," was all Chrissy could utter as she got closer. "You guys *built* this?"

"In fairness,"—Joe shrugged, tapping his hammer in his palm—"I've already built it once before, this is just a smaller version of it."

"Do you know what carol it's supposed to be, Chrissy?" Kevin asked. He encouraged her answer with a smile and quirk of his prominent brow. "I'm hoping it translates."

"Well, since this is a replica of the McHenry house, and you'll be at the helm this year, my best guess is *I'll be Home for Christmas*?"

"You most definitely are more than just a pretty face!" He gathered her into a hug that lifted her from the ground. He had a habit of doing that. "It's spot on, right? And I have that summer spent rebuilding your home to thank for my acquired construction skills."

"I'm glad it wasn't a total waste of your time."

"Chrissy, time spent with you could never be considered a waste." He flashed that disarming smile again. It made Chrissy uneasy at the way her stomach fluttered in response.

"I should find Nick. Looks like we'll be starting any minute."

"You guys did a good job with yours," Kevin offered, though the compliment wasn't a particularly glowing one.

"Thanks." Chrissy bowed out of the conversation and peeled herself from Kevin's appreciative gaze. "See you on the hill."

"You might not actually see us. We'll be flying by."

"Gotcha." She nodded and gave the father-son team a thumbs up.

It didn't take long to spot Nick with their sled. He looked up as soon as he heard her approaching. "Hey, Chrissy. I was beginning to think maybe you stood me up," he teased through an adorably lopsided grin.

"I did get a bit distracted by all of the sleds on the way in. I can't believe there are so many this year!"

"Right? Everleigh said there were close to twenty pairs entered in the race." He grunted a little as he pressed up from his crouched position. "I don't know. I still think we have a pretty decent chance with this trusty old sled. It hasn't let us down in the past."

"I'm sorry I missed our opportunity for a trial run. I slept in later than I should have."

"No biggie. I don't think we need one, anyway. And I'm honestly not that confident that this makeshift creation will survive more than one run. But we probably should at least sit in it before we take it up the hill."

"Agreed. You first?"

"It'll work better if I'm in the back, if that's alright with you. That way I can help steer the end with my weight so we don't fishtail like that one year."

"Oh gosh. I'd forgotten about that! Remember how I panicked and overcorrected and we ended up doing a complete three-sixty? It's amazing we still won."

"It was especially slushy that day. People were skidding and dumping out of their sleds left and right. I think Marcie and Tuck even crossed the finish line backward. Today's layer of powder is going to help all of us out. Like a fresh, cottony slate." He motioned toward the sled with a lift of his chin. "Go ahead. Climb in."

Chrissy stepped over the cardboard flank, her boot hooking on the edge. The decorative bells jingled. "Sorry. I'll try not to completely ruin it." She lowered down and sat, shimmying up to the front.

"I brought duct tape. You're fine."

Hauling his leg over the side, Nick sank onto the sled, right behind Chrissy. His immediate presence at her back was expected, but the shiver it elicited was not. She slowly released a quiet breath.

"See those handles down by your feet?" Chrissy looked down. She saw them. "I added those this year so you have something to hold onto."

She angled her head, scoping out the remainder of the sled behind her. "Just one set? What will you hold onto?"

Nick moved his mouth close to her cheek as he slid his arms around her waist and said, "You."

Chrissy's breath whooshed out. "Right." How she managed a stutter on just one syllable baffled her, but it happened. "Makes sense."

"Let's test this out. Go ahead and lean left," Nick instructed. She felt his secure grip tug her gently to the side. She shifted her weight in response. "Good. Now right."

She leaned the other direction.

"Pull back."

Hesitantly, Chrissy pressed her shoulders backward, meeting Nick's chest like she was almost leaning on him. She was grateful for the puffy jacket she'd just purchased and the layers it provided between them.

"Great. I think we're ready." If he was as nervous as she was, he did a good job masking it. He lifted out of the sled and held a hand out for Chrissy. "We're in the second heat, so we have a little bit of time. Want to grab some hot chocolate and watch our competition from the sidelines? My treat."

"I think that sounds like a great plan. And Nick?"

He swiveled around. "Yeah?"

"Try not to scream like a little girl when we speed down the raceway. Last time my ears rang for a full week."

He reached in his pocket, pulled out a set of earplugs, and tossed them her direction. "Sorry, Chrissy. No promises."

NICK

❄

THE TIME TO beat was one minute, twelve
seconds.

Four teams were disqualified in the first heats. One
veered recklessly off the path, eventually coming to a stop
at the base of a hollowed out evergreen. Thankfully, no one
was hurt, other than a bruised ego or two. Another pair was
disqualified for illegal use of tinsel. Nick still wasn't sure
what that meant exactly, but it gave the remaining teams a
greater chance at the trophy, so he didn't delve too deep.
The third was cut from the competition after purposefully
ramming into an opposing sled and the last lost their spot
because one racer fell ill that morning and they swapped
out drivers without notifying the judges beforehand.

To his surprise, the *Jingle Bells* sled held its own and
only required a few minor touchups after the qualifying
round. Their official time was one minute, twenty-two
seconds, but Nick was confident they could shave off a

few seconds in the final race. He knew that his nerves didn't help the situation any and he hoped to get those under control the second go around.

It turned out a minute and a half was a long time to hold someone in your arms. Nick overthought every move, wondering if Chrissy focused on their closeness as much as he did. He couldn't read her reactions. She'd hunkered down deep in the front of the sled, her hair whipping out behind her like a cape, tickling Nick's nose and occasionally flying into his eyes which obscured his vision. Even still, Chrissy navigated well when he couldn't see clearly and they crossed the finish line with an impressive time under their belts.

"Looks like it's down to us, your dad and Kevin, the LOL's and Corey and Robert Taylor." Chrissy read the results from the leaderboard. "Too bad Tucker and Marcie didn't make the cut."

"I think they're okay with it," Nick said. "They both mentioned they needed to head over to the tree lot to open it up for the day, anyway."

"I wouldn't think they'd have much business until the races are over. Looks like the entire population of Heirloom Point is here."

"It sure does, doesn't it?" From the wreath auction to the sledding races, Nick was continually impressed with the town's supportive showing. "So, do you have any final suggestions for our next run?"

"I have one," Doris snickered as she sauntered up. "Try to keep up with us old gals."

"I thought you had more birds on you earlier this morning." Nick cocked his head, puzzled.

Doris glanced down at the flock of fake birds pinned to her holiday sweater. "I lost two turtledoves and a French hen up at the top of the hill. Nita's looking for them now."

"Those weren't real then?" Chrissy looked shocked. "Oh, thank goodness! I think we ran over one during our race and I've been feeling so guilty about it this entire time. I honestly thought I took out a tiny woodland bird!"

"You can take out all the birds you like, so long as you don't take us off the podium."

"Is it strange that I'm actually a little intimidated?" Nick whispered to Chrissy as soon as Doris was out of earshot.

"She talks a big game, that's for sure. But she's harmless. And if we can avoid any of her discarded fowl on the way down, I think we can increase our speed and lessen our time. The race is ours to lose at this point."

"I like your strategy." Nick thumbed his chin. "And Chrissy?"

"Yeah?"

"You got some kind of hair tie to put all that hair back in? I couldn't see for a while there."

Chrissy's hand flew up to her beautiful auburn mane. "I'm so sorry, Nick! I didn't even think about that!"

"It's no biggie." Then, smiling he said, "You still use the same apple shampoo from high school, don't you?"

A blush crept across her cheeks as she shoved her hand into her pocket to pull out a rubber band. "I'm a bit of a creature of habit," she admitted as she twisted the dark strands into a low ponytail at the base of her neck.

"Me too."

"Remaining racers!" Everleigh's voice broke into their conversation, magnified through the megaphone speaker. "Please begin hauling your sleds up the hill! The final race will take place fifteen minutes from now!"

Reaching down to grab the rope handle, Nick held it out for Chrissy to take hold, too. "What do you say we go crush some Christmas carol competition?"

❄

NICK BACKED HIS truck into the driveway and killed the engine. From his rearview mirror, he could see the garage door open, rolling up panel by panel to reveal Chrissy standing on the other side. Nick hopped down from the vehicle and rounded the bumper.

"Thanks for storing it here," he said as he hauled the sled out of the truck bed. They'd already removed the cardboard decorations as the snow did its expected job of turning it into a soggy, disintegrating mess. "I don't have a lot of storage at the rental."

"No problem. There's some room in the rafters if you think we can hoist it up there."

"Between the two of us, I bet we can manage."

Nick lifted the sled over his shoulders, shifting to get his footing right so he could manage the awkward weight of it. Steadying himself, he strode into the garage.

"Wait!" Chrissy called out just as he was about to

raise the sled higher to shove up in between the exposed beams. "We forgot something."

"What's that?"

Grabbing a pocket knife from a nearby workbench, Chrissy flipped it open. The blade swiveled out. "We need to carve another tally."

"How could I forget?" Nick lowered the hefty sled onto the bench. "Would you like to do the honors?"

"I think we both should." Extending her hand, she cradled the small knife in her palm.

"I think that's a great idea."

Nick took both her hand and the pocketknife and wrapped his fingers around the instrument. Then, holding onto the knife together, they etched another groove into the wooden slat. Chrissy rested her hand on Nick's a moment longer as they looked at the tallies.

"Five wins. Not too shabby," she said.

"Not at all. I think we really lucked out with the LOL's ultimately getting disqualified. I had no idea you had to cross the finish line with ninety percent of your decorations still intact."

Chrissy snickered. "I think by the time they finally made it down the slopes, they only had eight days of Christmas represented on their sled. I'm certain we passed at least four golden rings and an entire partridge in a pear tree on our way down."

"All they had to do was ask to borrow some duct tape. I would've shared."

"Right, but then I think we'd be sharing the title, and this is one I'm happy to have the only claim to."

"Me too, Chrissy."

Letting go of his hand, she looked down at the garage floor and then smoothed her palms on the thighs of her pants. "Nick, thanks again for agreeing to do this with me. I know it was out of your comfort zone, but I had a lot of fun. Felt like a kid again, actually."

"I did, too," Nick said. The butterflies, the adrenaline.

"I suppose it's only fair that I agree to attend the dance with you, then. Step outside of my comfort zone a little, too." Her smile was tentative, like she wasn't fully confident in wearing it.

"The dance?"

"The Heirloom Point Winter Ball? Next Friday night? I got the invitation."

He wasn't sure what invitation she referred to, but he saw *this* as an invitation to spend more time with Chrissy, and he wasn't about to let that opportunity pass him by.

"Oh! Right. The ball," he said, nodding, like it merely slipped his mind for a moment. "So, would you want to go?"

"I think so. But it's been a long time since I've been to a dance, Nick. I'm not sure I even remember how."

"I'm in the same boat. I think we just have to remember that—unlike this morning's adventure—a dance isn't a competition. Just an opportunity to dress up and have a good time."

Relief relaxed her features. "I don't even know what to wear. I don't have a dress fit for a ball. Looks like I'll have to do a little shopping between now and then." The growing grin she wore indicated she wasn't too upset about that fact. "What about you? Did you ever need anything fancy when you were out on the road?"

"I have a couple nice suits from the times I had to attend benefits or other publicity functions. They're still in storage, but I've been thinking it's probably time I ship out the rest of my things from Newcastle."

"Really?"

"Yeah. There's no real sense in keeping an empty apartment in a city I'll likely never set foot in again. And my things are just collecting dust in storage, anyway. It'll be good to have all the pieces of my life back in one place."

"That's a pretty big decision, Nick," Chrissy said, "to decide to come home for good."

"It might be a big one, but it's an easy one."

❄

"I BROUGHT YOU a housewarming present." With arms outstretched, Chrissy shoved a small green gift bag over the threshold and into Nick's hands.

"You didn't need to do that." He took the bag and stepped aside to allow her in. "I've lived here almost two weeks already."

"I know, but it's the first time I've seen your place and showing up empty handed doesn't feel right. It's just a candle, anyway. Nothing big."

"No such thing as just a candle if it came from your shop." He reached his hand into the bag and pulled out the scrunched tissue paper surrounding the jar, then tossed it to the floor. His place was a mess already, strewn with large brown boxes that were dropped off a few days earlier. He'd eventually clean it all up once everything was unpacked. "An Heirloom Christmas," he read from the festive label. Unscrewing the lid, Nick raised the jar to his nose. "This smells so good." He took another breath. "Wow."

"You're officially the first to own one. I'm putting them out in the shop tomorrow morning."

"Well, I'm honored, Chrissy. Let me grab a match and find a place for it." He paced to the kitchen and withdrew a book of matches from a drawer before striking one on the side of the packet. The matchstick flared to life and he passed the flame off to the wick. "I really like this scent. It reminds me of all the things I love most about Heirloom Point. How did you manage to wrap all that into one candle?" he asked rhetorically. "Amazing. Thank you for this, Chrissy. It's great."

"You know what else is great?" The front door flew open, the handle ricocheting off the wall, and Tucker appeared. He held two cardboard pizza boxes high in the air. "Dinner! I brought sustenance in the forms of pepperoni and pineapple. I hope you're hungry."

"I know I am." Everleigh shoved around Tucker. She uncoiled her scarf and slipped her jacket from her shoulders, then dropped them onto the back of the couch. "Let me have at that Hawaiian pizza. My favorite!"

"Sis!" Chrissy rushed over. "I didn't know you were coming."

"Many hands make light work and by the looks of it, Nick could benefit from a few more hands. Or an octopus. I've never seen so many boxes in one space before. Just how big was your apartment back in Newcastle?"

"It was pretty big." Nick opened a cupboard and pulled down a stack of plates and plastic cups, and then got a two-liter of soda out of the refrigerator. "Honestly, I was never really there, so it was a waste to have that much square footage and that much in rent. If I had been a little wiser with my finances, I might be in a different position right now."

"Maybe so, but we wouldn't all be together, sharing the holidays and this piping hot pizza. I know I'm not just speaking for myself when I say I'm glad you decided to come home, Moose."

Fanning a slice of pizza with her hand, Everleigh blew out a cooling breath and then agreed, "It's like old times, just with a lot more baggage." She swiveled her gaze around the room. "Seriously, where do we even start?"

"Anywhere you can. Most of it is probably junk anyway, but it'll be good to sort through."

"You know the saying: one man's trash is another man's treasure," Tucker said.

"Yeah, but sometimes one man's trash is still just garbage. Feel free to toss anything you think I won't need. I doubt I'll even miss it."

CHRISSY

CHRISSY POURED HERSELF a cup of coffee and pressed her hands to the kitchen island. It took great effort to keep her gaze fixed out the window over the sink and not on the newspaper clipping resting on the counter next to her.

There was so much joy outside in the forms of newly constructed snowmen and inflatable Christmas yard decorations and the laughter that floated on the air as young children threw snowballs at their siblings in the hopes of getting in a surprise shot. The sky was cloudless, the streets full, and Chrissy knew her heart should burst with cheer but each time she reread the article, all of that joy whooshed out of her.

She'd managed to avoid Nick's calls and his presence for two days by saying she'd come down with a nasty cold and needed her rest. She even dodged his attempt to drop off homemade chicken noodle soup. She didn't want

Nick to catch her illness just before the dance. He bought the lie and graciously gave Chrissy her space.

But she hated lying to him. It felt so unnatural. Reaching for the mug, Chrissy sighed and dumped the coffee down the sink drain. The strong drink wouldn't do anything to calm her already twisting stomach. Likely, it would only make it worse. Instead, she pulled two pieces of bread from the tin breadbox and dropped them into the toaster. When they jumped up in their slots minutes later, she flinched, even though she'd been expecting it. Her nerves were rattled, her spirit weary.

She buttered the bread while the toast was still hot in her hands and the pads melted quickly. She would force herself to choke it down. She needed to take care of herself so she didn't actually fulfill the fabricated lie about being under the weather.

She wondered if being physically sick and being heartsick were that much different after all. It felt the same, that heavy fog settling in, the urge to stay curled up under the covers rather than face the day, the craving for peace and quiet and solitude.

Against her better judgment, Chrissy snagged the article for her morning reading material and plated the toast to take to the dining table. Maybe another read through would clarify things. She had skimmed it half a dozen times already, hoping the words would rearrange on the page to form something new. Something that didn't crumble her confidence. Unfortunately, with each read the letters became more fixed in their positions than ever, and their meaning became even more engrained in her heart than she thought possible.

She fought the betraying smile that pulled at her lips when she took in the black and white portrait of a young Nick. He was baby-faced and courage-filled. Only now could she recognize this look as hope. For his career. For his future.

She held a bite of toast in her mouth as she read the article.

Who is Nick McHenry, the Newest Power Forward for the Newcastle Northern Lights?

You've probably noticed him on your television screen this season, both his large, imposing size and quick maneuvering ability making him a leader in points and penalties. Twenty-one-year-old Nick McHenry may play a tough game on the ice, but what do we know about the other areas of his life? Newcastle Tribune's Fiona Boyle sat down with the handsome, rising star to learn a bit more about his future in the rink (and in romance).

Chrissy smoothed the crumpled paper, skimming over the introductions that contained information she already knew about Nick. Things like his favorite foods, pregame rituals, and how old he was when he first laced up his skates. She skipped down to the last paragraph.

FIONA: We're all dying to know, Nick, is there a special someone in your life?

NICK: Currently? No.

FIONA: So that means there used to be? Can you tell us a little bit about her?

NICK: I didn't necessarily say there used to be someone, just that there isn't anyone now. I'm here to focus on hockey and to give my all to the Northern Lights. I've been given a once-in-a-lifetime opportunity to play for the team I've loved since I was a little kid and I'm so thankful for that. I'm living my dream.

FIONA: Seems like you're good at skating around more than just the ice. So, no love interest?

NICK: You're really not going to let this go, are you?

FIONA: Nope. You can block my attempts all you want, but it's my goal to get this out of you.

The news reporter was relentless. Chrissy could envision Nick squirming in his seat and hear his nervous laughter and she stifled a snicker at that visualization.

NICK: Okay, so there was someone back at home but we're no longer together.

FIONA: Care to tell us about her? I'm sure there are a lot of single ladies who would love to know what your type is.

NICK: I wouldn't say I have a type because ultimately, we ended things. She was just what I *needed in that time in my life but as we all know, things change.*

FIONA: Sounds like it was pretty serious?

NICK: At the time I thought it was, but life has a way of creating opportunities and showing you the path you're supposed to take. The one with her wasn't where I was ultimately headed.

FIONA: Do you regret anything when it comes to that relationship?

NICK: I probably regret more than I should.

FIONA: Well, I know I'll regret it if I don't ask you one last burning question: Where do you see yourself in ten years?

NICK: Still on the ice, hopefully. Traveling. Making a name for myself in the hockey world and giving back to the sport that gave me everything.

FIONA: Well, I think you're well on your way, Nick. Thank you so much for taking the time to give us this interview. We wish you success in all of your endeavors and have a feeling we'll be seeing the name Nick McHenry around for a long time to come.

NICK: I hope you're right. Thank you, Fiona.

Crumpling the paper in her hand, Chrissy tossed it across the room, not feeling the slightest bit of guilt over damaging the old article. After all, Nick had used the newspaper as wrapping for his hockey trophies and other breakable items like salt shakers and measuring cups. It wasn't under protective glass and framed like some of his other newspaper clippings.

The only reason Chrissy even saw it was because Nick's picture stared up at her when she opened the flaps on the cardboard box. At first she thought she'd stumbled upon a treasure, this decade-old news piece about an up-and-coming hockey great. But as the saying reminded her, it was only trash.

Deep down she couldn't stomach the thought that Nick regretted their relationship. The ring slipped onto her finger—even though temporary—had indicated otherwise.

There were years and years of good times and only a few moments of bad. It was easy to bury the bad under the memories that would always make her smile. The night Nick told her he'd signed the contract with the Northern Lights started off as a celebration. This was his greatest dream finally becoming reality. It felt like the biggest win for them both.

But when she stepped out onto that front porch, two glasses of lemonade in hand and a naïve hope in her heart, Chrissy sensed things were about to change. It was the only time she had ever seen Nick cry, and the tears flowed before his words did. It scared her, honestly.

By the end of that night, he'd broken their engagement, along with Chrissy's heart.

❄

FROM THE OTHER room, Chrissy could hear the trill of an incoming text. She hoped it wasn't Nick checking on her again. She wasn't sure how much longer she'd be able to keep him away. At some point, he'd stop by unannounced. She was certain of it.

Luckily, the text was from her sister.

Everleigh: *We're about to sell out of your Christmas candle again. Everybody loves it! Only four left on the shelf.*

Chrissy: *I'll come by tonight and make some more. Thanks for letting me know.*

She watched the text bubble on the screen, knowing her sister was composing her reply. Within seconds, her phone pinged again.

Everleigh: *Why don't you come down this afternoon instead? We can go for a walk and get some fresh air. Nita can manage the shop on her own for a bit. Maybe we can even grab a coffee at Jitters?*

Chrissy: *Still not feeling well. Should stay home and get some rest. Thanks, though.*

Everleigh: *You're a terrible liar. I know you're not sick.*

Chrissy: *Sure I am. Cough, cough. Sneeze, sneeze.*

Everleigh: *What on earth did you find in those boxes that's got you so messed up, sis?*

Chrissy blinked back the tears that collected as she typed the words that trembled out from her fingertips: *The truth.*

NICK

❄

H E HADN'T TIED a necktie in years. Nick's hands struggled to recall the muscle memory. It took three fumbling attempts, but soon he had a knot tucked just under his crisp, white collar.

Not too shabby, Nick thought as he appraised himself in the mirror. Thankfully, his tailored black suit still fit, despite his recent absence at the gym. He'd borrowed a festive green and white plaid tie from his dad, along with a crimson pocket square that he tucked neatly into place. Shaking out his arms, he breathed deep.

He hadn't seen Chrissy all week. She'd been ill and was thoughtful in her avoidance, but Nick didn't worry about catching anything. All he wanted was to care for her. Multiple times he'd offered to bring over a meal or run by the pharmacy to pick up a prescription, but Chrissy shooed off his efforts. He even threw out the idea that they could skip the dance altogether and stay in. They could watch a marathon of holiday movies; there were hundreds to choose from. Bake gingerbread cookies. Attempt to redecorate Chrissy's tree.

She didn't bite at any of the suggestions. Nick began to worry she would cancel on the dance completely, so when Chrissy texted that morning, asking if they could meet at the community center rather than her house, he didn't even feel the disappointment he had every right to. Of course he would have preferred to pick her up at her place; it would make it feel like the date he hoped it was intended to be. But everything about their recent interactions hinted at a cancelation, so the fact that they were still on for the ball was music to Nick's ears.

He'd been humming Christmas carols all morning, laughing to himself at the new meaning many took on. Nick would never be able to sing *The Twelve Days of Christmas* without a bird-clad Doris coming to mind. He loved that he had only been home a short while, but the memory-making was well underway.

At a quarter to six, he headed across town to the dance. Just weeks before, the community center boasted hundreds of auction wreaths hung on the walls for display. Tonight the space was once again transformed. A half-dozen, ornately-dressed Christmas trees stood tall throughout the room, each a different holiday theme. There was a candy cane tree, all red and white, sparkling splendor. Another was a woodland winter theme with birds and nests, antlers and decorative feathers. Nick thought he even saw a few repurposed items from the LOL's sled tucked in. There was a tree that he knew his father surely had a hand in. Measuring tape wound around the girth of it as garland, various tools and metal gadgets clung to the branches, and he recognized the twinkling lights as the same they'd used the day before as a scarf for their newly constructed Slushy.

The best parts of Heirloom Point were on display and it was a beautiful sight.

Nick couldn't help but appreciate the dedicated citizens who made the holidays the most wonderful time of the year. From Everleigh and her leadership at the sledding race, to the notably hard-working Winter Ball committee, to the Tuckers with their tree farm and Miss Sandy with the auction. Even Chrissy had her candles dotting the center of each round table placed throughout the hall. There was an opportunity for everyone when it came to hometown tradition and Nick couldn't wait to find his rightful spot.

"Moose!" Nick felt a heavy palm come down on his shoulder. "You sure clean up well, buddy." Tucker handed his friend a cup of punch and grinned. "Almost didn't recognize you."

"The same could be said for you," Nick retorted. Tucker looked great in his umber wool vest and matching bowtie.

"Every now and then I pull out my dancing shoes and polish myself up. Especially if there's a chance that I'll get to dance with a beautiful girl."

Nick followed Tucker's directing gaze across the room and when it landed on Everleigh, he almost did a double-take. Like her sister, she had always been pretty, but tonight she could be the belle of the ball. Her blonde hair was swept into an elegant updo, her bright eyes dusted with iridescent glitter, and the pale blue, empire dress she wore twirled out from her slim waistline like cascade of icicles. She was stunning.

"I don't think I've ever seen anyone so beautiful in my entire life," Tucker muttered, unreservedly awestruck.

Nick was almost about to agree when Everleigh stepped aside.

"Wow," Tucker gaped. "I might have to take that back."

Just beyond her sister, arrayed in a rich, emerald green strapless gown, stood Chrissy, sipping from a flute of sparkling cider. Her auburn hair hung loose at her shoulders in tumbling curls and the rouge of her cheeks and deep, rose-colored stain of her lips made her look like Christmas come to life.

Nick lost his breath.

"You'll have to pick that jaw up off the floor." Tucker chuckled, noticing the captivated look of his friend. "Someone's going to trip."

Nick clamped his eyes shut and tossed his head back and forth, attempting to shake the trance. He didn't want to be caught gawking, but he'd never seen Chrissy look so striking. They'd attended prom together in high school, but they no longer looked like those love struck kids. They were all grown up in appearance and age, and Chrissy was hands-down the most beautiful woman Nick had ever laid eyes upon.

"She looks like she's feeling much better, doesn't

she?" Tucker asked, but Nick had stopped listening. He'd already begun making his way across the crowded room.

"Okay, then," Tucker said, but his words were swallowed by the holiday music that circled around them. "Guess I'll catch up with you later."

Nick wasn't sure how he would greet her, if the words would lodge dryly in his throat or if they'd spill out in a blubbering, indistinguishable jumble. He had every instinct to just take her hand and sweep her onto the dance floor to spend the evening wrapped up in each other's arms and in conversation.

"Dance with me." Nick was abruptly cut off in thought and motion. Doris Beasley grabbed his elbow, determined and insistent as she hauled him to the center of the massive room. "All Earl's interested in is the shrimp cocktail and that cheese platter. But I'm itching to cut a rug. Care to be my partner?" She swung her arms out to the side and tapped her toes along to the jazzy Christmas melody.

"Not sure I can keep up, but I'll try."

"Don't worry. I'll lead."

"I didn't doubt that for a second."

Doris took one hand firmly into her grip and reached up to place her other on Nick's shoulder. "I might have to stand on your feet, Nick. You've gotten so tall. Then again, I might be shrinking."

Nick looked down at Doris. She was dolled up in a fluffy white stole with a red jumpsuit underneath and sequin-studded ballet flats on her tiny, elfin feet. "Maybe it's a little of both," he said with a wry grin.

"Probably," she agreed. "I'm a little surprised you're not dancing with Chrissy already."

"It's definitely on my agenda."

"Well, that's good to hear. She looks beautiful tonight, doesn't she?" Doris swiveled and peered around Nick's shoulder. "Like a Christmas princess."

"I don't think I've ever seen anyone more radiant in my life." Nick tried not to gape. "Hard to believe she was sick all week."

He felt Doris's weight shift in his arms. "Don't think she's been sick, Nick. She came into Jitters just a couple days ago after she made another batch of her Christmas candles. Can you believe she's sold out twice already? Not that I ever doubted it. She's so good at what she does; there's really something special about this year's fragrance. An Heirloom Christmas is what she's calling it," Doris rattled on as they rocked back and forth to the up-tempo beat. "Anyway, she was the picture of health last I saw her."

"I was under the impression she was in bed all week with a head cold. That's what she told me, at least."

"Not sure why she'd tell you that."

As they made another rotation around the dance floor, Nick caught Chrissy's gaze, holding onto it until Doris had them spinning back toward the long spread of food where her husband stood, a full plate of appetizers in hand. Earl tipped his chin toward the duo and then placed his hors d'oeuvres onto the banquet table before he advanced their way.

As the song faded into the next, Nick stepped out of

Doris's embrace, offering a half-bow. "Thank you for the dance, Doris, but I think someone would like to cut in."

"Looks like seeing his ol' girl in the arms of another man was all the motivation he needed to put down the cheese. Thanks for the dance, Nick. I might steal another one from you before the evening is over."

"I'll be saving one just for you, Doris."

The hall was more crowded now and Nick had trouble seeking out Chrissy. There were couples parading around the room, arms linked as they admired the decorations or made pleasant small talk with neighbors and friends. Chrissy had been swept up in the melee and it wasn't until Nick did a full revolution around the community center that he spotted her in the middle of the dance floor, already swaying side to side with someone else.

"In fairness, I think she was hoping you would ask her first." Everleigh sauntered up behind Nick. She pulled a cherry from her drink and popped it into her mouth. "Looks like Kevin beat you to it."

"Really? I figured she was just being polite and didn't want to get me sick," Nick remarked, but he didn't like the bitterness woven in to his words. "I'm sorry. That was rude."

"Not any ruder than making up a fake illness to avoid a confrontation."

"What confrontation?" Nick shook his head. "That's what I don't get. Why would Chrissy need to avoid me? Did I do something wrong?"

Sympathy crossed Everleigh's gaze, tightening her

brow briefly. She set her drink down and popped open her clamshell purse. Pulling out a faded piece of newspaper, she passed it to Nick. "This might re-jog your memory."

"What is this?"

"An article. Chrissy found it when we helped unpack your things earlier in the week."

"And she kept it?" Nick turned the page over in his hands. "I don't even remember giving this interview."

"Then you probably won't remember saying you regretted your relationship with her, either."

Nick's eyes flashed. "I've never said that."

"Skim down to the end." With a pointed finger, Everleigh tapped near the paragraph in question.

Wildly, Nick's eyes raced across the paper. Bits and pieces came back to mind. It had been one of his very first interviews after he was drafted and the reporter was a particularly aggressive one. She seemed much more interested in his availability than his talent, which, as an athlete still trying to prove himself on the rink, was a little insulting. In the end, Nick felt like he had held his own and he'd been happy with the final news piece, even if it was admittedly fluffy. Is wasn't something he would ever put on display, like the articles that boasted championship wins and titles, but it wasn't something he was totally ashamed of, either.

"I still don't see where it says I regretted our relationship."

Everleigh snatched the paper back. "Question: *Do*

you regret anything when it comes to that relationship? Answer: *I probably regret more than I should."*

Nick yanked the article out of her hands. "Yes, like not making her my wife by walking her down the aisle! That's the regret I'm talking about here, Everleigh. Not that I regretted the relationship. I regretted *ending* it!"

Everleigh's mouth rounded into an *Oh* shape. "Well, that changes things a bit. But can't you see how she might have interpreted it differently? You said life showed you the path you were supposed to take and Chrissy wasn't on it."

"Right. I know I said that, because it was what we both agreed on at the time. My path was hockey. Chrissy's was here in Heirloom Point. If we married, she'd be forced to follow me around while I chased my dreams rather than follow her own. That's not something I could ever ask her to do, to sacrifice her future for mine."

"I'm not sure that was articulated very well in the article."

"I guess I've learned to articulate my feelings a little better over the years."

Suddenly, Everleigh grabbed Nick by the shoulders and swiveled him in an about-face. "You might want to articulate those feelings to Chrissy soon rather than later, because it looks like she's dancing her way to the mistletoe and I think Kevin may have plans to articulate something of his own."

CHRISSY

KEVIN WAS A great dancer. His footsteps were smooth and his carriage confident, but Chrissy couldn't allow herself to relax in his arms. In fact, she couldn't keep her ears tuned toward their conversation or her gaze focused on his light green eyes that kept dipping down to hers, asking for connection.

"Chrissy?" Kevin stopped dancing. "Hello, Chrissy? You with me?"

"Yes?" She snapped her eyes up, startled by the sudden pause in movement. "I'm sorry. Did you say something?"

"I said you look gorgeous in that ball gown. Green is definitely your color."

She blushed, not from the compliment, but the fact that she'd forced him to repeat it, her attention completely elsewhere. "Thank you, Kevin. You look great, too."

"I wasn't sure if you'd be here tonight, actually. Nick says you've been pretty sick."

"I was, but I'm feeling much better now. Just a head cold that took some time to shake."

"Well, I'm glad to hear you're on the mend. I can't say this ball would be nearly as enjoyable without you on my arm."

Placing his hand low on her back, Kevin drew her close, steering them through the twirling couples on the floor. Holiday carols played by the jazz quartet guided their movements and, for a brief moment, Chrissy wished she hadn't made so many excuses over the years. The Winter Ball was certainly an event worth attending and dancing with Kevin should be an effortless way to ensure a good time.

Why couldn't she allow herself to fall for someone like this man? Someone who clearly admired her and wanted to pursue a relationship with her. Kevin wasn't quiet in making his intentions known and there was a relief in that, if only for the fact that she knew where he stood.

Chrissy had no clue where Nick stood anymore.

"It's a little crowded right here," Kevin said with his mouth pressed into her hair, speaking loudly enough to be heard over the band. Within the stretch of one eight count, he spun them out from the middle of the room toward the decorated trees at the periphery. Chrissy could see the mistletoe dangling from the ceiling above, its leaves and red ribbon a siren call to young lovers hoping to steal a Christmas kiss.

Sometimes she wondered what it would be like if she would just allow herself to move on. Maybe kissing Kevin wouldn't be such a bad thing. If she kissed him, then maybe the feelings would magically follow. Maybe you didn't always need to be in love with someone to explore the idea of a future with them. Maybe this misguided belief was her great mistake of the last decade.

"Chrissy, I know I head back just after Christmas, but..." Kevin swallowed. His head lifted and his eyes intentionally angled upward. "But I'd like to spend the remaining time I'm here with you." He pursed his lips. "I really like you, Chrissy. I have for some time now and I think you might like me a little bit, too. If you'll just let yourself."

The confession- though not surprising—threw her into a tailspin. The room began to pirouette around her and she struggled for focus. "Kevin, I—"

"Hey, brother. Mind if I cut in?"

Kevin's spine pulled taut like a snapped wire. He narrowed his gaze and glowered over his shoulder, the interruption evidently an unwelcome one. "I do, actually. Chrissy and I aren't quite done here."

"It's okay, Kevin. We can share another dance later," Chrissy assured, patting his arm.

Dejection fell heavy onto Kevin's strong features as he reluctantly shrugged out of their embrace. He gave his younger brother a telling look before turning back to Chrissy. "Okay. But save the last dance for me. And please think about what I just said."

"I will," she agreed as she stepped into Nick's arms.

"Thank you," she said quietly as she placed her hands onto Nick's shoulders.

"I didn't mean for this to be a rescue mission," Nick teased, "but once I saw where you were standing, I figured I needed to jump in."

"It's not that I don't like Kevin—"

"Chrissy, you don't need to explain anything."

"But I feel like I should. He's a good man, Nick. And I know he's interested. I've just never thought of him that way. I guess I always felt like I shouldn't feel that way about anyone until"—she held her breath a beat before she added—"until I was over you."

"Chrissy." Nick's chest puffed up with a large inhale. "I owe you an explanation."

"No. I owe you one. I wasn't sick—"

"I know."

"Wait—you knew? How could you know?"

"Doris told me. And you don't really look like you've been sick in bed all week. In fact, Chrissy, I've never seen you look so radiant. You're breathtaking."

His words made her stomach flip, like she'd crested the highest peak of a rollercoaster. After such a sweet compliment, she felt almost guilty confessing the reason for her lie, but she had to be honest with him. It didn't do anyone any favors to continue this charade.

"I was avoiding you, Nick, but more than that, I was avoiding my feelings," Chrissy acknowledged as they spun out from under the mistletoe and onto the dance floor teeming with couples. "I read something that I shouldn't've when we were unpacking your things.

About how you regretted being together. I was so hurt at first. In fact, all week I was angry and frustrated and couldn't understand how something that was so special to me could be something that you wished had never happened." Chrissy tore from their stare and blinked back the insistent tears that fought to spill their way down her cheeks. She focused on Nick's impeccably knotted tie instead as she added, "You are allowed to have your regrets, Nick. We all are. But I'm also allowed to cherish that time we shared—that time we were so very much in love—even if it ultimately meant different things to each of us."

Although the song quickened and the other dancers adjusted their movements to match the new tempo, Nick and Chrissy slowed to a near stop right in the center of the room.

"I have never regretted loving you, Chrissy." Nick's voice was wrought with emotion as he drew her close, his arms binding around her fully. "*Never*. The only regret I have was in letting you go. I don't even know what a different scenario would have looked like for us—if you would have come on the road with me or if I would have stayed with you here—but I do regret leaving you. *That's* my big regret. I regret not following through on my promise to marry you and build a life and a future with you, Chrissy." Nick's feet shuffled again, guiding them back into a swaying motion that resembled a dance, but it was clear neither were focused on their steps. "I don't know what it is about holding you in my arms that makes me say these things so freely. I think I'm just afraid to let you go again without telling you just what you mean to me, Chrissy. What you've *always* meant to me."

"Honestly, Nick, I spent all week rehearsing what I was going to say and none of it involved admitting that I've never gotten over you." Chrissy shed a small smile. "So I guess we're even."

She looked into his hazel eyes, flecked with golden specks that had always captivated her so. Nothing had changed about the tender warmth they emitted and nothing had changed about the way they made her heart instantly soften and bend toward his.

"I hope it's clear I'm not over you either, Chrissy." Ever so slightly, he pulled her a touch closer. "I think I just didn't know how to tell you that. I didn't know how to get back to where we once were. All I've wanted to do since coming home is to relive all of the memories from our past. Like maybe we could fall in love all over again if we did. I think maybe that's why I waited until the holidays to come back. They always were our favorite time of year."

"Is that the reason you left the notes?"

"What notes?"

"The notes in the wreath I won from the auction. Notes about meeting at the tree lot and the coat drive." She squinted up at Nick, though his face was void of comprehension. "How you asked me to be your partner for the sledding race and invited me to the ball?"

"Those weren't from me, Chrissy." Then, laughing a little, Nick said, "But that would've made things a lot easier if I would have thought to do that."

"The notes weren't from you?"

"No, they weren't."

"Then who were they from?"

"I'm not sure, but it sounds like maybe they came from someone who hoped to spend more time with you." Nick's eyes darted across the hall toward his brother who stood at the food table, chatting with Tucker and Everleigh as he popped a sugar cookie into his mouth.

"They couldn't've been from Kevin." Chrissy read Nick's thoughts. "They started before he even came into town."

"Maybe they are magical notes," Nick teased as a lopsided grin spread onto his face. "Okay, maybe not magical, but at least notes meant to draw us back to one another."

"I can't think of anyone who would do that. No one cares that much about whether or not we pick up where we left off."

"Really?" Nick asked as his eyes quickly swept over the room. "I can think of a few people who might."

Following his gaze, Chrissy caught sight of Doris and Earl who were both beaming at them, snooping unabashedly as they circled the floor. There was Chrissy's dad with Miss Sandra on his arm, throwing a quick salute to his daughter from his post by the entrance doors. There was Marcie who rose up on her toes to toss a wave to the couple. And there was Tucker and Everleigh, about to join them on the dance floor, grinning broadly like they knew some secret that Nick and Chrissy didn't.

"You think one of them had a hand in the notes?"

"It's a theory, I suppose." Nick shrugged. "But you know what's not a theory and is an actual fact?"

"What's that?"

"That I'd love to share the next dance with you. And maybe the one after that. Probably the one after that, too."

"Oh Nick," Chrissy teased right along. "I thought you'd never ask."

"I've got about a decade's worth to catch up on, Chrissy. I sure hope you brought your dancing shoes."

NICK

❄

NICK'S HANDWRITING WASN'T the best, but Chrissy assured him no one would critique his penmanship. He had arrived at Chrissy's candle shop just before opening, even though the Winter Ball had lasted well into the late hours of night. The replayed conversations, the many dances, and the hope that unfurled at the thought of a budding relationship with Chrissy kept Nick awake until almost dawn. Even with little rest, he was eager to start the day, if only for the fact that he'd be spending it with Chrissy.

It took the two no time at all to pen the perfect prose. Nick was quite pleased with their final composition.

Christmas Eve comes but once a year,
So let's share a meal and some holiday cheer.
There's warmth in our hearts and snow on the ground,
All that's left is for our friends to gather 'round.

It's Chrissy and Nick's great Christmas wish
That you'll join them on the 24th with your favorite dish.
Be sure to include the recipe to share
And wear a sweater with some holiday flair!
We'll eat and chat, dance and mingle
And have a merry ol' time like we're jolly Kris Kringle.

"I think if this whole candle business doesn't work out, you could have a very lucrative career as a greeting card creator," Nick quipped.

"What can I say? I've been inspired by my wreath." Chrissy surveyed the unfolded notes on the table. She hadn't noticed it before, but each undoubtedly had a different author, the nuances and curves of the letters and words varying on every sheet of paper. "Your idea to bring a recipe is brilliant. We can use those for comparison. You're quite a sleuth, Nick."

"Yes, but it only works if they handwrite them and don't type them out."

"I'm confident they'll be handwritten. Pretty sure Nita and Doris don't even own computers."

"I don't know. Those LOL's are pretty hip," Nick said, then added with a mischievous grin, "In fact, I just heard Doris recently had hers replaced." He paused as he acknowledged his failed attempt at humor. "Not my best joke, I'll give you that. Anyway, Christmas Eve is just two days away. Are you sure I can't do anything to help you get ready for the dinner? It's no small feat to host that many people for a sit-down meal."

"Apart from helping me place the invitations in the

wreaths, I can't think of anything. I'll make a holiday ham and you can bring the green bean casserole we talked about. I think it will be a wonderful night. And hopefully, by the end of it, we'll be one step closer to discovering the author of these mystery notes." They looked to the front door as Nita opened it, arriving to begin a shift. Chrissy lifted her hand in a wave and then returned her attention to Nick. "I know it shouldn't really matter who they're from, but I can't help but feel there's some greater meaning behind them. And to think I thought I was bidding on a plain, ordinary wreath."

"Nothing about Heirloom Point is ordinary, least of all its people. We'll get to the bottom of this. I, for one, am all about solving a good mystery. They don't call me Nick 'Sherlock' McHenry for nothing."

"They don't call you that."

"Okay, but they should. Has quite a ring to it."

Chrissy chuckled. "Alright Sherlock, let's grab our coats and set out on our mission. Should we drive or are you okay with walking?"

"The weather's great and my knee's cooperating. I vote we walk."

Nick also knew it would take much longer on foot, which inevitably meant more time together.

"I'll just touch base with Nita real quick and then we can be on our way. Meet you outside in five?" Chrissy asked.

"Take your time."

Nick tipped his chin toward Nita as he slid by her and out the door. From this side of Spruce Street, he could see the recently constructed snowman that he had, with his father, created a few days earlier. With the sudden rise in temperatures, the bottom portion had already begun to melt, creating puddles on the sidewalk at the base of the figure. Nick made a mental note to clean it up that afternoon. He didn't want anyone slipping, potentially injuring themselves.

When the door creaked behind him, he turned, filing that task away for later.

"All set." Chrissy slid her arms into her jacket and then handed the stack of notecards to Nick. "I'm so thankful for Nita's help with the shop this year. She's both a great employee and friend. Plus, I think she really enjoys working here."

"I think it would be hard not to enjoy being surrounded by candles all day. It's like having hundreds of potential wishes right at your disposal."

"You know, I've never made a wish on any of my candles."

"No? Only on candles stuck in cakes? Just birthday wishes for you?"

"Christmas wishes, too. But I'm still bitter about my ungranted wish from Santa all those years ago. I'm tempted to track him down, just to inform him that you're never too old for a little Christmas magic."

"I think if you tracked him down, he might have a question or two about that stolen cap. Best to leave that thievery in the past."

"I suppose you're right." Chrissy's shoulders lifted in a shrug. "So, where should we start?"

"Your dad's place and the Beasley's are closest—I say we head that direction and then hit the others when we circle back. We can make one big loop if we plan it out right."

Slipping her hand into the crook of Nick's elbow, Chrissy leaned close. "Thank you for playing along with me, Nick. I really do appreciate it."

"You're welcome, but I'm not playing along. I'm just as curious as you are about the meaning of these notes. In fact, I just might have to thank whoever is behind it all. If the intended purpose was to bring us back together, I'd say it's working."

He felt Chrissy press deeper into his side, confirming his hope that she entertained the idea of a future with him, too. No question about it, thank-yous were definitely in order.

❄

NICK STARED AT the sterile, white wall, focusing on the clock hung near the ceiling. He watched the second hand that ticked in sync with his heartbeat.

"The nurse said the doctor should be by any minute." Chrissy pulled back the partition and then gently sat down at the foot of the hospital bed after she slid the curtain closed behind her. Even with her cautious movements, Nick winced as the bed dipped. "He's going over the x-rays right now."

"I'm so sorry, Chrissy. I'm sure this is not how you

planned to spend your afternoon. Honestly, I'll be fine here if you want to take off."

"Right. Like I'm going to leave you all by yourself when it's my fault we're here in the first place."

"It's not your fault."

"Yes, it is. I was the one who thought I saw someone in the Beasley's front window. If I hadn't panicked, you wouldn't've rushed down those steps and slipped on that black ice. I take full responsibility."

"If I didn't slip there, I would've slipped somewhere else. I'm really not that great with balance these days."

Chrissy grew serious. "Nick, I had no idea your knee was causing you this much trouble. I wish you would have been honest with me about that. We could've driven. I wouldn't've suggested we walk, had I known."

"I wanted to walk with you, Chrissy." Nick thought back to the first few blocks they spent arm in arm and how that eventually progressed to hand in hand as their stroll carried on.

"Nick McHenry?" The curtain rings scraped on the rail again as a doctor pushed them aside and stepped into Nick's hospital room. He extended a hand that Nick took into his own. "Nice to meet you, Nick. I'm Dr. Timmons and I'm a big fan. Big fan."

"As in hockey?"

"Absolutely. Our entire family loves the sport and the Northern Lights are our team. I even bought my son your jersey for Christmas two years back. He slept in it every night for a solid year, until he outgrew it."

Sure, Nick had received fan letters over the years, but

he still had a hard time believing there were kids who looked up to him in the same way he had admired his hockey idols. It was a humbling reality he had never quite gotten used to.

"We were all sad to hear your contract ended, and after looking at your x-rays, I'm even more disappointed."

Nick's heart sunk. He figured his knee would always give him grief, but having the doctor imply that the end of his hockey career had been inevitable released the last shred of hope.

"It's okay, Dr. Timmons. I've come to terms with the fact that my hockey days are a thing of the past."

The doctor's eyes narrowed behind wire rim glasses. "I wouldn't say that at all, Nick. The opposite, in fact. From what I can see, you've healed very nicely from that original injury."

"But it's caused me a lot of discomfort recently."

"That's understandable. It's a great deal colder here in Heirloom Point than it is in Newcastle. Has it mostly been stiffness that's been bothering you?"

"Yes. Stiffness and the occasional shooting pain."

The doctor nodded. "That's all to be expected. You're not at one-hundred percent yet, but certainly getting there. There's going to be some nerve sensitivity in your joints due to scarring, and that's aggravated and worsened as the temperatures fluctuate."

"So the pain I've been experiencing is normal?"

"There's not really any such thing as normal with these sorts of sports injuries, but let's just say I'm not all that concerned about a bit of pain here and there. I would suggest wearing a brace so you don't continue to reinjure it like you did today. And if the pain does become too intolerable, there are medications we can prescribe that will help manage your comfort. I'm hopeful you can expect to see a continual and gradual improvement. I wouldn't completely rule out your days in the rink, either," Dr. Timmons said. "I know our high school hockey team could sure benefit from some solid coaching."

Even if the doctor had written it out for him on his notepad, Nick wouldn't be able to process this information any easier. "You don't think I should stay off of the ice?"

"Were you ready to leave it?"

"Honestly? I'm not sure I know the answer to that question."

Holding his clipboard against his chest, Dr. Timmons crossed his arms and tilted his head thoughtfully. "I think if you love something, there's always a way to work it into your life. You don't have to give up your dream completely, just start dreaming it in a different way." He smiled down at Nick as he added, "You're an incredibly gifted hockey player, Nick, and I think your talents are a real gift to our town. If it's your goal to get back out on the ice, then let's make sure that happens. For now, take it easy, keep your weight off of it, and let your body continue to heal. I'll send Carol back in with a set of crutches for you to use over the next week and then she'll get you discharged so you can get out of here and enjoy your holiday."

"Thank you, Dr. Timmons. I appreciate not only the medical advice, but the life advice, too. I didn't realize how much I needed it."

"Happy to help, Nick," the doctor said. "You take care and you both have a very merry Christmas."

"Same to you."

They waited a moment in silence after the doctor left. Then, as though out of nowhere, Chrissy erupted in laughter.

"What's so funny?"

She snorted, then covered her mouth to conceal it. "I love how you said your nickname was Sherlock, when I believe Old Man Winter is much more fitting."

"He basically did just say it's weather-related joint pain, didn't he?"

Chrissy pulled out her phone and swiped on the screen.

"What are you doing?"

"Deleting my weather app. I won't need it anymore with you around," she teased as she stowed her cellphone back in her purse. "You'll let me know when you feel a storm a' comin', won't you?"

"Oh, I see." Nick smiled. "You've got jokes now, too, huh?"

"I can't let you have all the fun." Chrissy placed a hand on Nick's forearm and left it there.

"In all seriousness, I'm pretty relieved right now. I don't think I ever let myself acknowledge how disappointed I was that I couldn't play hockey again. And now it looks like that might not be the case. Did you hear what he said about the hockey team? That would be incredible to give back to the school that helped me get my start." Nick breathed out, feeling his entire body relax. "For the first time in the last year, my future has never felt so bright."

Chrissy squeezed his arm affectionately and the smile that drew out her dimples was warm and full of optimism and hope. "Mine hasn't either."

"PEPPERMINT WHITE MOCHA," Doris called out as she placed the drink onto the bar.

"Thank you, Doris." Chrissy took the cup and then slid it into a cardboard sleeve. She pressed her mouth to the rim, pulling in a minty sip. "I need my caffeine fix before I head home to finish cleaning the house for tonight's dinner."

"Thanks again for the invite. Earl and I are really looking forward to it. I'm bringing potato casserole and a fruitcake."

"I thought you didn't like fruitcake?"

"Not all fruitcake. Just that awful one you gave me years ago," she said as she straightened the cups and lids on the counter near the espresso machine. "I'm bringing the recipe so you'll have a chance to redeem yourself when it comes to holiday baked goods in the future."

"I think I'll just stick to candles that smell like baked goods and leave the actual baking to the others." Chrissy rotated the coffee in her hands. "Thanks for the mocha, Doris. It's delicious. Like Christmas in a cup."

"Speaking of Christmas." Doris nodded toward the entrance of Jitters as the door opened and another patron stepped out of the snow flurries and into the warm sanctuary of the coffeehouse. There, in all of his North Pole glory was Santa Claus, or at least the man who dressed up as him each year for the town's many holiday functions.

Chrissy studied him. He was the best Santa she'd ever seen with his plush red suit, black leather belt, and thick boots that looked like they'd been worn more often than just once a year. He was hands-down the most realistic Saint Nick around, his presence both believable, yet inexplicably magical all at once.

"He's really good, isn't he?" Doris acknowledged. "He's here for the afternoon for any kids who want to come by to share their Christmas wishes. We had planned to set up his sleigh outside in the square, but the weather's too unpredictable lately." She looked across the café. "Do you think you could help me move that high-back chair closer to the fireplace? I think that'll be a good place for him to set up shop."

"Absolutely," Chrissy said as she put her drink back on the counter and waited for Doris to round it. The two women then slid the large velvet chair toward the hearth and stepped back to survey the scene. Wrapped presents with perfectly tied bows were stacked off to the side and stockings were hung on the mantle with the names of each of Doris's employees embroidered on them. It was a cozy and inviting space. "This looks great."

"Doris," the man greeted as he walked over and engulfed her in a mighty hug. His voice was rich and full. "How have you been since I saw you last?"

"I would say I can't complain, but we all know that's not true," Doris admitted, much to Chrissy's surprise. "I can always find something to complain about," she added, snorting. "Santa, this is Chrissy."

"Hi, Mr. Claus." Chrissy played along. She held out her hand to shake his which was covered in a pristine, white glove. "Glad to meet you."

"Oh, I do believe we've met before." The man lifted his other hand to his long white beard to stroke it gently. Chrissy took note of the way it stayed securely on his chin and didn't pull like a fake beard would. This Santa was definitely a good one.

"If you've been in the business of playing Santa for a while now, I'm sure we have met," Chrissy said as she reached to take another sip of her mocha before it cooled to an unfavorable temperature.

"Gosh, I've been Santa for as long as I can remember," he said, his apple-round cheeks lifting in a massive grin. "I might look a little different to you now, though. Long ago, I had a different cap."

A blush of embarrassment spread up Chrissy's neck and onto her face. "I...um..."

"It's okay, Chrissy. The missus made me a new one." He flicked the puffy white ball attached to the end of his cap and it jingled like a bell. "The last one didn't do that," he said with a wink.

"I'm so sorry. I'm happy to return it. Believe it or not, I still have it."

"That won't be necessary, Chrissy. I just wish you wouldn't have raced off so quickly all those years ago."

"You said I was too old to make a Christmas wish. I overreacted and hurried off because I was so embarrassed."

"What I had said was you're *never* too old to make a Christmas wish." The man looked down at her with empathy full in his twinkling eyes. "Sometimes we hear what we are expecting to hear instead of what is actually being said."

The old newspaper article and the recent misunderstanding with Nick popped into Chrissy's mind. She let out a quiet laugh as she shook her head. "I seem to have developed a bad habit of doing that."

Reaching into a large sack slung over his shoulder, the Santa pulled out a scroll and handed it to Doris. "Would you be able to find a place to hang this for me, Doris?"

"Yep. There's room right next to the fireplace," she said as she unrolled the paper. There, in flawless calligraphy, was a catalogue of names with the words *Santa's Nice List* written neatly across the top.

"Do they send you to some sort of penmanship school to learn to write like that? It's impeccable," Chrissy noted, awe infiltrating her voice. She wished her handwriting was even half as good.

"Something like that," the man said with a grin. "I sure do hope you ended up getting your wish, Chrissy."

"I have—or at least I think I'm in the process of it. Just a few years after the fact."

Leaning close, the man whispered, "Sometimes Christmas magic doesn't work on the same timeline we do."

"Speaking of timelines," Doris interjected with a shout, "we need to get you situated before the kids show up. We've got ten minutes until this place is filled with rugrats, all clamoring for a chance to climb onto your lap and tell you their laundry list of Christmas wishes. Let's get moving!"

❄

"THAT HAM SMELLS amazing." Nick hobbled into Chrissy's kitchen, struggling with a casserole dish in hand and a crutch tucked under each arm. "I let myself in. Hope that's okay."

"Of course. And I'll pass that info along to Crocker's Grocer—all I did was pop the ham into the oven to warm it up. They did the rest."

"Either way, it's got my stomach growling. Where should I put the green beans?"

"On the counter is fine."

Chrissy untied the apron from around her neck and rubbed her palms together. It wasn't often that she hosted her neighbors for dinner and she was beginning to wonder if she had possibly bitten off more than she could chew with the task at hand.

She flipped her wrist over to look at her watch. "Is it really 6:30 already? People should start arriving any minute."

"I just saw your dad pulling into the driveway when I came in."

At that moment, Chrissy heard her father's voice call out from the foyer, the creak of the front door swinging shut behind him. "Merry Christmas!" he bellowed, and when he rounded the corner into the kitchen, Chrissy wasn't at all surprised to see Sandra at his side, just like she had been the night of the Winter Ball. It looked like Lee had taken his daughter's words to heart about dating again and Chrissy couldn't be more pleased. No one deserved happiness more than her father.

"Hi all," Sandra said as she thrust a foil-covered baking dish toward Chrissy. She seemed unreasonably nervous, her smile forced and voice shaky. "I made some apple streusel."

"Thank you, Sandra. I'm really happy you could make it tonight. This smells wonderful." Chrissy wrapped Sandra in a hug, hoping to ease the woman's nerves. "And I'm glad you're keeping an eye on this guy." She raised her eyebrows in her father's direction. "Someone's got to keep him in line. It's become a bigger job than Everleigh and I can handle on our own."

"I have to remind him that even though he enforces the law, he's not actually above it."

"Alright ladies, I'm happy to see you two getting

along so well, but can't an old man catch a break?" Lee turned to Nick. "What do you say, buddy, should we crack open a drink?"

"Right this way." Nick tipped his head and used his crutches to help him maneuver over to the refrigerator.

Within the span of an hour, Chrissy's home had completely transformed. Crockpots, bowls, pie tins and platters littered the kitchen island, half-filled with what remained of the holiday dishes and desserts her guests provided. The dining room was a cacophony of conversation, multiple discussions held around the large table all at once. She could hear the faint track of Christmas music playing through the surround sound speakers and it provided the perfect backdrop to such a joyous night.

Chrissy and Nick had yet to even think about collecting their guest's recipes to study their lettering. That particular task was on the backburner for now. All she cared to do in the moment was share this beautiful evening with her friends and family during the most wonderful time of the year.

When she had first purchased the Miller place, she had visions of nights like this unfolding within the walls of her home. She wanted it to be a space of laughter and enjoyment, and for the first time since signing the mortgage papers, it was exactly that.

"Did you ever think there could be this much noise in your house?" Nick pressed his shoulder to hers as he spoke. He took a napkin and wiped his mouth, then placed it back onto the table. "I can barely hear myself think over all the chatter."

"I had the hope it would be. It gets awfully quiet here all by myself."

"I know the feeling. Life on the road could be a bit isolating. It was almost strange how I craved the roar of the stands, if only for the assurance that I wasn't alone."

Chrissy took Nick's hand into hers, resting it on the table between their place settings.

She couldn't ignore her sister's raised eyebrows from across the room, her gaze flitting to their interlocked fingers. Chrissy also picked up on Doris's appreciative smirk and knowing nod. The sudden display of affection didn't appear to come as a surprise to her friends and Chrissy was thankful for their quiet approval.

"What do you say I help you get the dishes started?" Nick asked, unaware of the eyes on them. "It's almost nine and I don't think our guests have plans to wrap up the evening anytime soon. They might need a subtle hint." Nick scooted back his chair, but kept his fingers woven with Chrissy's. Only at the last minute when he pulled the crutches from their resting place against the wall, did he let go of Chrissy's hand.

"Let's leave the dishes." Then, locking eyes with him, Chrissy added, "And let's leave the guests for a bit, too."

"You lead the way."

Chrissy guided Nick through the dining room and out into the sitting room at the opposite end of the house. The conversations faded as though a volume dial had gradually been turned down until they were finally alone in silence.

"I love this view," she said as she looked out through

the huge picture windows. The many cars parked just outside her home didn't clutter the street, but rather hinted at a house filled with company and that was profoundly comforting to Chrissy. "This is our town and these are our people, Nick. Even if we don't solve our little mystery tonight, I think it has been a success. Just having everyone I love under one roof is all I could ask for this Christmas."

Nick looked like he was about to speak, the words right on the tip of his tongue, when his gaze fell to the coffee table next to them. "What's this?" He reached for a folded notecard as he balanced with his crutches under his arms and read aloud:

*We were asked to bring the recipe of our favorite dish
But we have a different Christmas wish.
We've known you both for many years
So we hope you'll take this advice from your
Heirloom Point peers:
There are lots of ingredients when it comes to love,
But the first step is to lift your eyes and look above.*

"Looks like they beat us at our own game, huh?" He rubbed the back of his neck with his hand as he glanced up toward the sprigs of mistletoe hung directly overhead. "I think they were onto us with that whole recipe thing."

"Looks like," Chrissy agreed. "I guess we didn't need to compare notes after all. It seems like everyone is doing their best to make sure we end up back together, doesn't it?"

"It would appear that way." He shuffled closer and Chrissy could feel his breath on her mouth as his lips parted to speak. "What about you, Chrissy? Is that what you want? For us to end up together again?"

Lifting up on her tiptoes, Chrissy let her answer be known with her hands curled around Nick's neck, pulling his face down to hers. As if he'd been waiting an entire decade for her answer, Nick dropped the crutches to his side, sending them clattering and skittering to the hardwood floor below. With abandon, he tugged her close to his chest, his full lips meeting hers in a desperate kiss that Chrissy felt deeper in her being than any of their past kisses combined. They were all grown up now and the feelings that bubbled up within her as their lips moved were enough to bring tears to her eyes.

With the lights from the tree twinkling behind them and the sudden rise of applause coming from the hallway next to them, Nick and Chrissy shared a kiss under the mistletoe, wrapped in each other's arms and lost in one another's affection.

"It's about time!" Chrissy heard Tucker shout, followed by a whoop of laughter. Chrissy slid out of Nick's embrace and looked toward her friends.

"I knew you two were always meant to end up together," Doris piped up. "I just knew it."

"All you needed was a little help to find what was right there all along," Everleigh said, her words calling back to the day in the candle shop. "And I, for one, was happy to be of help."

"Me too," said Kevin, stepping around the crowd

gathered in the hall. He walked over and placed a hand on Nick's shoulder. "You've got a keeper there, brother. Don't do anything to mess this up a second time around."

"You know I won't," Nick said, his eyes never leaving Chrissy's. "Not a chance."

Over the next half hour, the guests began to filter out, each acknowledging how happy they were for Chrissy and Nick and their renewed chance at love. Her father was the last to leave, and he held Chrissy in his arms just a bit longer than usual.

"You both have always had—and will always have—my blessing," he said to Chrissy and Nick who stood hand in hand in the foyer. "A second chance at building a life together is a precious gift."

"Don't I know it," Chrissy said, squeezing Nick's hand. "I won't take it for granted, Dad."

"Oh!" Sandra, who had already walked out the front door and was waiting on the porch, suddenly twirled around like a spinning top. She dug frantically within her purse and then, once finding what she was looking for, handed a piece of paper to Chrissy. "I think this is for you. I've been meaning to give it to you for some time now, but kept forgetting."

"What is it?"

"You know that wreath you won? It was left on the front door of the community center on the day of the auction. I just figured it was from someone who didn't get theirs turned in in time. And this was the note that was tucked into it. I think it might help explain how one simple wreath turned our little town of Heirloom Point into a community of merry matchmakers."

Chrissy waited until Sandra and her father left before opening the note. She closed the door and turned to face Nick, her eyes alight with intrigue and wonder.

"Should we read it?"

"Is that a real question?" Nick's chin pulled back. "Absolutely!"

Sliding her finger in between the pages, Chrissy flipped it open. Her breath instantly caught when she saw the exquisite calligraphy and read the following words:

It started as an unspoken wish many years ago
And took nearly a decade to grow.
But this magical wreath is where the new story begins
Where two past loves find their way back again.
They might need some encouragement as the days go by
to remember their past and give love another try.

"Do you know who wrote this?" Nick pulled the note from her hands and examined it as though looking for some sign of authorship.

"I think I just might," Chrissy said. "Someone told me today, in fact, that you're never too old for a Christmas wish. I think this note and my wreath just might finally convince me of that truth."

"Do you happen to know the wish it's referring to?"

"I do." Chrissy placed a quick kiss on Nick's lips

before saying, "But if I tell you it, then it might not come true. And I, for one, really want this wish to come true."

Leaning in for another kiss that was deeper and more heartfelt than the last, Nick pulled back only briefly to say, "If it involves getting to spend the rest of my life here in Heirloom Point with you, then you're free to keep that wish to yourself. Just know that I'll be wishing it right along with you."

EPILOGUE

NICK AND CHRISSY

"YOU'LL FEEL A little wobbly at first, but don't be scared. I'll be holding onto you the whole time. I won't let go until you're ready."

"Like when you taught me how to ride my bike?"

"Just like when I taught you how to ride your bike."

The weather was ideal for the first week of December. Not a cloud in the sky, only a refreshing chill that made heavy jackets and scarves a necessity. It wasn't quite the same as his hockey gear, but it provided a similar, comforting indicator of the changing of seasons.

Glancing toward the edge of the frozen pond where Chrissy sat on a fallen log, Nick caught sight of her in a puffy, thick jacket with their son bundled close to her chest. She pulled the knit beanie down over the toddler's ears and called out across the ice, "You're going to do great, Audrey. Daddy's the best ice skater I know. You have the perfect teacher."

"Daddy's the best *everything*!" Audrey hollered proudly, her words whistling through her gapped grin.

"Yes, he is." Chrissy gave her husband a smile that, even after six years of marriage, still caused his heart to flutter.

Nick looked down at his other favorite girl with that same sense of awe, excited for today's milestone. He took Audrey's small, mitten-covered hand into his. "Okay. Here we go. We're going to push off with our left foot first, then our right."

Audrey's legs began to quiver, the skates etching grooves in the top layer of ice as she struggled to stay upright. She lifted a heavy skate and shook it. "This one?"

"Your other left."

"You're silly, Daddy. I don't have two left feet."

"Sometimes I feel like I do. Especially when I'm dancing."

"Ohhh! I want to dance!" Audrey's eyes sparked with delight. "Let's dance!"

"But we're learning to skate right now, sweetie."

"We can dance with our skates on. I've seen it on TV before. Is that the kind of skating you used to do on TV, Daddy?"

"Not quite." He chuckled. "But if you want to dance, we can dance. There's *always* time for dancing." Stooping down, Nick scooped up his young daughter. She threw her arms around his neck and squealed with delight as he whipped around Prosper Tomlin's pond, spinning and twirling as the winter wind kissed their reddened cheeks.

"I feel like a princess!"

"Because you are, sweetheart. You're Mommy and Daddy's princess."

"Just like in the fairytales?"

"Just like in the fairytales."

Audrey grabbed ahold of Nick's face with her chubby, little hands and pressed her forehead to his, trapping his gaze with her bright blue eyes. "Tell me the fairytale about you and Mommy again. It's my favorite."

"The one with Santa and his town full of helpers?"

"Yes! And the magical notes and Christmas wishes."

Nick spent the next several loops around the ice telling his daughter about the time the prince came back to Heirloom Point and fell in love with the princess who had always held his heart. He shared of a Christmas wish made by a beautiful young girl that took over a decade to come true. And he told of their happily ever after that included two little miracles, one named Audrey and the other named Jack.

"That's the bestest story ever, Daddy."

"It sure is. And do you know why?"

"Because it's true," Audrey said, nodding, knowing she had the right answer because it was the one he'd always told her.

"Exactly. Because it's true."

※

"JACK IS ASLEEP in Grandpa Lee's arms upstairs and Grandma Sandra is getting a fabulous makeover, compliments of Audrey. Looks like we are guaranteed at least ten minutes of quiet."

Chrissy fell onto the couch, swinging her legs up onto the cushions. The Christmas tree twinkled in her periphery and she laughed at the thought that it didn't look all that different from years back. The ornaments scattered across the branches now were made by a very crafty five-year-old and they rivaled Nick's salt dough designs in both construction and creativity.

"Was that the door?" Chrissy asked as she adjusted her position on the couch, trying to get comfortable.

"I didn't hear anything," Nick answered.

"No, I definitely think it was the front door. You should go check it out."

"Probably just the mailman. He can leave whatever it is on the porch." Nick stretched his legs out to prop his feet onto the coffee table as he lifted his arms high above his head, rolling out his shoulders. "Man, between practices with the team and today's time on the ice with Audrey, I'm really beginning to feel my age. Those high school kids skate circles around me and I have a feeling it won't be long at all until Little Miss is doing the same."

"I really think I heard the door," Chrissy said again, insistently.

Nick dropped his head back onto the ledge of the couch and closed his eyes, then sighed. "Okay. I'll go check, but after that, I plan on taking a nice, long nap, bordering on hibernation. You can wake me up when it's Christmas."

Pushing up, he strode to the front door and grabbed onto the handle, flinging it open wide. Just as he suspected, nothing was there to greet him other than a blast of winter air.

"I think you're hearing things, sweetie," he called into the house.

"What about seeing things?" Chrissy shouted back. "Do you see anything out there?"

Giving the porch a swift once-over, Nick shook his head. "Nope. Nothing."

"Are you sure?"

Then, turning back toward the door, Nick saw it. He reached into the wreath to retrieve the folded paper note. "I see what you did there," he said to himself, smiling.

What started as two soon became three
When we had our sweet little girl, Audrey.
Then Jack came along, making us four,
So what do you say we add one more?

Nick froze.

"Did you find anything?" Chrissy hollered after a stretch of quiet.

Snapping from his shock, Nick bounded back through the house, his footsteps loud as they clapped against the floorboards. He raced toward his wife who was laying on the couch and scooped her up into his arms.

"We're having another baby?"

"Yes," Chrissy said, unable to contain a giggle. "We're having another baby!"

He settled her back onto solid ground and placed a hand on her stomach. "How far along?"

"Four weeks. I just took the test last weekend."

"You've kept that secret from me since last weekend? So that's why you've been so quiet these last couple of days. And sleeping nonstop. Man, Chrissy, you are good!"

"I was worried I would let it slip and I really wanted to give you the big news by leaving that note. It was perfect, right?" She grinned, proud of her successfully carried out plan. "But in fairness, we *have* gone much longer than just a few days without really talking. I've had some practice."

Peppering kisses across her cheek, Nick paused and looked her in those bright blue eyes as he said, "That was the longest and loneliest decade of my life, Chrissy. Had I known that I had this beautiful life with you in store, I would have never left Heirloom Point."

"That's all in the past, Nick. Our future is all I ever want to focus on. You, me, Audrey, Jack, and our newest little one."

He met her mouth again in a sweet kiss, one that conveyed the great love he had, and always would have, for the only woman to ever hold his heart. "That's one dream I'll never lose sight of. Merry Christmas, love."

"Merry Christmas."

THE END

ABOUT THE AUTHOR

Growing up with only a lizard for a pet, Megan Squires now makes up for it by caring for the nearly forty animals on her twelve-acre flower farm in Northern California. A UC Davis graduate, Megan worked in the political non-profit realm prior to becoming a stay-at-home mom. She then spent nearly ten years as an award winning photographer, with her work published in magazines such as Professional Photographer and Click.

In 2012, her creativity took a turn when she wrote and published her first young adult novel. Megan is both traditionally and self-published and *An Heirloom Christmas* is her tenth publication. She can't go a day without Jesus, her family and farm animals, and a large McDonald's Diet Coke.

❄

To stay up to date on new releases, sales, and cover reveals, please sign up for Megan's newsletter:

http://subscribe.megansquiresauthor.com

To keep up with Megan online, please visit:

 facebook.com/MeganSquiresAuthor

twitter.com/MeganSquires

Did you know you can enjoy your very own *An Heirloom Christmas* candle?

Visit www.megansquires.com/candle to learn more!

Printed in Great Britain
by Amazon